More Praise for *A Floating Life*

"Talking bears, talking dogs, time travel, and a midlife crisis: Tad Crawford's brilliantly original and entertaining first novel, *A Floating Life*, brings South American magical realism to twenty-first-century America in a mesmerizing story of one man's search through the realms of myth, history, and the human psyche to explore love, friendship, family ties, vocation, and, in the end, what it means to live in an ultimately mysterious universe.

"Tad Crawford is an utterly fearless writer who will and does go wherever his wonderfully anarchic imagination takes him."

—Howard Frank Mosher, author of *A Stranger in the Kingdom*

"By turns charming and ominous, whimsical and philosophical, *A Floating Life* is a multilayered, shape-shifting miracle of a first novel."

—Melvin Jules Bukiet, author of *Strange Fire* and coauthor of *Naked Came the Post-Postmodernist*

"Throughout this fantastical saga of privation, like Odysseus's voyage without a homecoming, like Dante's tour without a guide or a Beatrice, Crawford's narrator recounts his amazing adventures in a mesmerizing diction of long-suffering cool.

"His losses are nearly total: spouse, child, occupation, property, potency, clothes (repeatedly), safety, and friends. In the end, in his memory and ours, we are left an account of magical encounters with imaginary creatures: a litigious dachshund, a terrifyingly helpful bear, a man called Pecheur who doesn't fish (men or fish). They cannot save him—often, indeed, they imperil him—but they can enchant our world. They did mine."

—Nelson W. Aldrich Jr., author of *Old Money*

"A haunting, unusual, sui generis, and wonderfully sustained novel that also manages to be hilarious. I loved it."

—Nick Lyons, author of *Spring Creek*

"Equal parts science fiction, magic realism, and hard-boiled detective story, *A Floating Life* is a dizzying journey through a fragmented landscape of ideas deftly rendered into a seamless, spellbinding narrative.

"Juggling the humorous, absurd, and stunningly profound, Crawford pulls off a nearly impossible feat: penning a page-turner that isn't afraid to show its smarts."

—Kenneth Goldsmith, author of *Uncreative Writing*

A
Floating
Life

A Floating

A NOVEL

Life

TAD CRAWFORD

ARCADE PUBLISHING • NEW YORK

Arcade Publishing books may be purchased in bulk at special
discounts for sales promotion, corporate gifts, fund-raising, or educa-
tional purposes. Special editions can also be created to specifications.
For details, contact the Special Sales Department, Arcade Publishing,
307 West 36th Street, 11th Floor, New York, NY 10018 or
arcade@skyhorsepublishing.com.

Arcade Publishing® is a registered trademark of Skyhorse Publishing,
Inc.®, a Delaware corporation.

Visit our website at www.arcadepub.com.

10 9 8 7 6 5 4 3 2 1

Library of Congress Cataloging-in-Publication Data

Crawford, Tad, 1946–
  A floating life : a novel / Tad Crawford.
    p. cm.
  ISBN 978-1-61145-702-5 (hardcover : alk. paper)
  ISBN 978-1-62872-422-6 (paperback : alk. paper)
  ISBN 978-1-61145-827-5 (ebook)
    1. Magic realism (Literature) I. Title.
PS3603.R3977F58 2012
813'.6—dc23

2012024097

Cover design by Mary Belibasakis

Printed in the United States of America

For
Susan and
Christopher

1

To see the celestial unicorn is to gain divine wisdom. Touching that shining horn heals every ailment. Diseases vanish, poisons are made powerless, and lost parts of the body grow back with vigor. Heroes, sages, adventurers of all sorts seek the unicorn. And yet they call the divine beast invisible, a creature of the mind, a myth. Let lesser men beware their choices, hesitate before challenges and journeys. The ocean depths, the caves within the earth, the dark fastnesses of endless forests, and the typhoons that rend the air bring death to all but the great. In foreign lands beyond the reckoning of our maps, I shall succeed where all others have failed.

From the log of Cheng Ho, admiral of the western seas, voyage of the fifth armada

2

The one-eyed man's kindly dark-brown pupil was surrounded by creases in his skin that I imagined had been shaped by smiles and looks of concern. He could have illustrated an ad for the miracles of plastic surgery, because his lone eye looked out from the center of his forehead without any hint of scarring from an operation. A tall man, close to seven feet, he wore a towering white hat to mark his authority over the dozens of people sweating before ovens, boiling pots, and frying pans. Waiters balancing trays rushed in and out, and I savored the scent of the delicious cuisine and wondered how the Mafia could employ such an expert chef to run this extensive kitchen.

The chef shed his white apron and hat and gestured for me to follow him. Dark hair grew in furry clusters on his naked body, and I realized that I too wore nothing. I must have forgotten to dress when I left the apartment that morning, but I had no recollection of waking, looking in drawers and closets for clothes, or even of my usual breakfast of milk and cereal. Fortunately, no one gave us a second look as I hurried after him in the busy excitement of the kitchen. He led me through a door, down a hallway decorated with scenes of gondolas and ancient buildings reflected in the water that would one day swallow Venice like a large fish preying on a smaller one, and at last opened a frosted glass door and brought me into a steam room with benches of worn marble.

Hot, billowing mist filled the room. I could see the bottom half of a man of more normal size dipping a wooden ladle in a bucket and pouring water that sizzled on the scalding rocks in a heater. A white splint covered his right forearm, and he poured with his left hand. The chef picked up a white towel, and I did the same. When he sat on the towel instead of wrapping it about his waist, I did that too.

"Comfortable?" asked my host.

"Yes, I'm fine," I replied, feeling the heat draw sweat from every pore. The other man had stopped wetting the stones and vanished into the steam on the highest level of the marble seats. The chef and I remained on the lowest level. I could see his eye studying me through the clouds of steam.

"I hope you don't mind the informal surroundings."

"Not at all," I assured him. I wanted to be agreeable and make a good impression, although I wasn't certain why.

He rubbed one hand over his large jaw with its dark stubble of whiskers and the other over the glistening bald dome of his skull.

"You know why I like it here?"

"It's a nice room," I said, not wanting to show that I had no idea. "Very old, elegant . . . "

"Because it's like the kitchen."

"Yes."

"Hot. I've come to like the heat. I've spent my entire career in what might as well be a furnace. Hot as hell," he said with a grin. "But what you have to realize is that after a few years, you don't feel it the same way. You acclimate. What once seemed scorching becomes comforting and familiar. The nice thing about the steam room is that it's quiet."

"Not as hectic as the kitchen," I said.

"It's a good place to consider things."

"Yes?" I tried to be affirmative, but I could hear the question in my tone.

"Yes, all sorts of things." He closed his eye and squeezed his forehead in his hand. "There's so much to think about, and it's not always clear. But you know this."

"What are you thinking about now?" I asked.

"Of course, your dossier for one thing."

"My dossier." The odd-sounding word made me uneasy. It belonged to bureaucrats, apparatchiks who cared only for the great machine of the state.

"I reviewed it carefully. I appreciate," he said with a nod of his head, "the thoroughness with which you filled out our questionnaire."

I couldn't remember filling out anything.

"You don't have the dossier here?"

"No no. It's kept with the files. The key point is that you want the job."

"Of course," I answered, concealing that I didn't know what job he meant.

"To be second-in-command is no easy thing."

"Ha!" This jeering interjection came from the man hidden in the steamy heights.

The chef waved an open palm to show that I should ignore the intrusion.

"Why is it," he asked, "so difficult to be second?"

"Everybody wants to be the boss," I said.

"Do you?"

What answer did he want? I couldn't take long to respond, because he would see my uncertainty.

"At the right time."

"Oh my!" This from the invisible man above us.

"And what time is this?" the chef asked encouragingly.

"Time for a change," I said.

"Yes, certainly. You wouldn't be here otherwise. And I am sorry to hear about your troubles."

"Which troubles?" I asked.

"At work," he nodded, "and at home too."

"I'm hoping for the best."

"Good, very good. And how long have you been interested in this position?"

"Since I first heard about it."

"How did you hear about it?" he asked.

"I listen very carefully."

Did I see the brow above that single eye wrinkle in the briefest frown? Had I jeopardized my chance of getting the job? I couldn't be sure, but he continued.

"What did you feel when you imagined applying for the position? When you had the fantasy of actually being a member of our staff?"

"It was a thrill I can't quite describe. And, to be truthful, I was a bit afraid, because the position is challenging. I know I can do it, but something new and important like this frightened me."

"How many years were you at the CIA?"

I hadn't the faintest idea, but I had to answer.

"The limit."

"That's good. What did you like best about the training?"

"I can't imagine a more thorough training. Everything was covered, and I mean everything," I repeated, stressing the word.

"In particular, what in your training prepared you to be a sous-chef?"

Then I realized that "CIA" referred to the Culinary Institute of America. I had visited the school once, many years ago. I hoped I could use the little information I recalled to my advantage.

"I know innumerable recipes by heart. Of course, I'm able to oversee efficient meal preparation and presentations for large parties."

"Are you sure? Even if the executive chef is occupied by his other duties?"

"Yes, on my own." An irresistible thought occurred to me, and I added, "In fact, the executive chef on board the ship suffered from seasickness. I often had to take full charge of the galley. And on those tour ships, we served more than five hundred people in a sitting."

"What ship?" He looked alarmed. "You didn't mention any ship in the questionnaire."

Would one lie cost me the position? I had never worked on a ship, but the specificity of the seasickness made me feel compelled to speak.

"Where did the questionnaire ask about ships? I don't remember that part."

"You had to fill in your work history. Of course, it didn't say anything about ships in particular."

"That's it, then."

"That's what?"

"My mind is very literal. If you say 'to purchase and guide the preparation of meals for a thousand people,' that's what I do. I don't worry about the bigger picture. For example, I wouldn't be thinking whether the dining room belonged to a world-class restaurant, a cruise ship, a college cafeteria, or a soup kitchen for the poor. I would only be thinking about ingredients. How will I get them? What will they cost? When can they be delivered? Is my staff on hand sufficient for the task? Can we meet our deadline? On and on like that. That's why I work well as the second-in-command. You, as the executive chef, might have a far larger view of the whole process, but at least I can be counted on to get my work done."

"You seem to have a fascination with ships." The chef frowned and a sullen pout inflated his lips.

"I do like ships," I said, not seeing how this could do any harm.

"He likes ships!" The voice from above returned, loudly and derisively.

"We don't like water here," the chef said fiercely, his eyelid blinking in a nervous shudder.

"But what about the steam?" I asked, with a dreadful sense of everything having taken an unexpected turn for the worse.

"Making water into steam demonstrates the power of heat," said the chef. "Boiling water is no problem. We have certain objections to ice, but at the bottom of it all the frozen wasteland has much in common with the burning desert. So we serve our sodas and alcoholic drinks in tumblers brimming with ice cubes."

"What if a customer asks for a glass of water?"

"For reasons of commerce," the chef replied with disdain, "we serve the glass of water. However, the heart of the kitchen is fire. Fire allows us to prepare our alligator in sauce piquante, our roasted hazelnut-marinated ostrich in shitake mushrooms, and our tuna with turnips in saffron sauce. Fire is the great transformer, the engine of change. When you ask to work in my kitchen, you enter the cauldron. When the fire has done its work, only the essence remains."

For the first time, doubt entered my mind. Did I really want this job? The chef's beliefs struck me as . . . unusual, even extreme. I wasn't certain what he meant or where this might lead. I tried to remember my current job, the office where I went every day. Nothing came to mind, but surely I worked. Whatever my job, it might be better than this. However, the chef's manner changed.

"It's always good to have a frank exchange of views," he said with an avuncular smile.

"Yes, of course."

"And he did us a good turn," said the voice of the hidden man in the top tier.

"Yes, you've already helped us out," the chef agreed. "We have a long memory when it comes to people who help us . . . "

"And also people who get in our way," added the voice from above.

"What makes you want to leave your present position?" the chef asked.

"After going a long way in a certain direction," I answered, "I want to explore more of the compass."

"But you're an account executive. Not an unimportant position. And to switch from a marketing agency to cuisine, even with your credentials from the CIA . . . You have to admit it's unusual."

He made me aware of some important facts. I could barely imagine myself as an account executive at a marketing agency, but I must have said this on the questionnaire.

"I'm not excited in the way I was when I started. To be part of a well-run kitchen, that would be different. It's the smoke and mirrors that I can't stand. How can bolstering this product or that ever make a difference?"

"He wants to make a difference!" The voice above us repeated my words with contempt. "Soon he'll want to make the world a better place."

"Working from recipes, even inventing some of my own," I went on without letting the unseen speaker disturb me, "overseeing the cooking and serving of artfully arranged dishes, contributing to nourishment and pleasure—that's what I want to do."

"Yes, I could be convinced that you're the one," the chef said with a shine in his eye. "But, tell me, do you have any questions for me? About what we do here? Or the benefits of the position?"

"I am curious about the benefits, and the salary of course."

The chef gave a careful list of the benefits, which included vacation, sick days, personal days, holidays, unforeseen weather days, unspecified emergency days, and a lot of other things to which I paid less attention. These included details of plans for health insurance, workers' compensation, disability insurance, and unemployment insurance. Perhaps they could protect me against every risk, but would any of these plans improve my life today, this instant?

The chef caught the drift of my unspoken thoughts.

"The life insurance, of course, would go to your wife. Enough to give her peace of mind and security during a difficult time of grief and transition. Unless, of course, you'd rather designate a different beneficiary. I know from your answers to some of the more . . . private parts of the questionnaire that your married life isn't all you might hope."

"I don't see what bearing that has on whether I'm offered the job."

"Enough of that," the chef said with a heartiness that I found contrived. "Any more questions about the position?"

"I would be the only sous-chef?"

"You mean the only second-in-command?"

"Yes."

"Absolutely. Our kitchen doesn't require more, though you'll have to use delicacy with the pastry chef. In the official hierarchy, you would rank above him. But we don't want him feeling out of sorts while he works on his confections. You might think of him as the ruler of his own domain, although his pleasures are ultimately encompassed within our menu."

"Yes, I see what you mean."

"He sees." The derisive voice broke in. "He's eager for the role of second-in-command. Not a thought for the difficulties, for always being under somebody's thumb."

I had been in the steam room too long. The heat had siphoned away my strength. I felt light-headed. If I didn't leave soon, I might collapse. The chef peered into the steam, and I heard stirring on the uppermost marble bench. The man descended from the gray mists, naked as the chef and myself, a white towel in his left hand. Now that I could see all of him, I measured him to be about my height and weight. In fact, he had my general body type—muscular across the chest and shoulders but flabby around the middle. Nothing that a well-tailored suit couldn't conceal. He shaved his head. His face, indeed all his skin, had a paleness that might have been called angelic if not for a perpetual sneer that made him look quite nasty.

"What happened?" I asked, gesturing toward the splint.

"I had a fall. What's it to you?"

I decided to ignore his tone. "I hope it heals quickly."

"Do you mind keeping your sentiments to yourself?" he asked. "Just because my arm got broken doesn't mean I've lost my pride."

I noticed that the chef fell silent. The Mafia ran this resort, not just the restaurant, but the casino and hotel too. Even in my heat-induced daze, I suspected the man before me to be a capo, perhaps the boss of the whole complex. He looked to be between thirty-five and forty, my equal in age if little else. I didn't reply to him. The heat had sapped me, and I had no idea what I might say that would please him.

"So," the man continued, looking me up and down, "you're the one who scammed the power company?"

I nodded my head. Hard as it may be to believe, I'd forgotten that I had gone undercover to help the authorities. I couldn't remember which authorities, but they had connections to the power company and had helped me to lower the electric bills for the entire resort. This ploy had led directly to my interview. If I could get the position as sous-chef, there would be no end to the useful information I could gather and pass on to the authorities. Why I would want to do this I couldn't say, after such a long sweat in the steam room. What benefit I would gain also eluded me. At least I would be taking the side of established order, the rule of reason and morality, against men such as the one who stood before me.

"I could make you a lot of money," he said. "I have plenty of friends, big men in business. If I say the word, they'd jump to be your clients. They'll pay me a third of what they save in power bills. I'll pass a quarter of that on to you. You could be a very rich man."

He frightened me, a visceral chill that made me shiver in spite of the heat. He cared nothing for the law, only for himself and his will to have power and pleasure. To him I might as well be an insect, something to let live if useful and crush under-foot if not. If I didn't want to help, he might kill me without a second thought. If I did help him, I knew I would move in a downward spiral through scheme after scheme of his devising.

He reached out his hands to rest on my shoulders. As he drew closer, I could see the points of golden fire in his green-gray irises. He ran his hands up my slippery skin and began to rub the tops and then the bottoms of my ears between his thumbs and forefingers.

"He's afraid," the man called to the chef.

The words relieved me. Not what they meant, but simply to have sound in the room. I couldn't remember hearing with such clarity and intensity, but the heat had obviously altered my senses. He caressed my lobes a few moments longer. His gentle touch made the shells of my ears tingle with a pleasure that reached into the canals.

Stepping back, the man shook his head. I knew then that I wouldn't be offered the position as sous-chef. But to me his gesture meant more than that, as if he'd made some comment on my life and who I had become. Feeling his rejection, I lost my fear of him. Suddenly I wanted to enter his world and feel again that pleasurable touch on my ears. For a moment I believed that the authorities, with their familiar demands, offered nothing compared to his criminal schemes.

"Did you really think you could fool us?" he asked.

My usual glibness vanished. "I . . . I . . . "

"We have informants. We know more than you could ever imagine. And we have our ways of handling matters."

"I just want to change careers," I finally managed to say, uncertain how this naked man might harm me but convinced that I faced the gravest peril.

"I'm sure you want that. You probably want to fix your little marriage too, almost as much as you want to break it up. But I'm talking about what you did to me." He tapped an index finger to his chest. "We murder for less than that. So what do you say? The big companies pay a third of what they save, and I pay you a quarter of that. Have we got a deal?"

I had been so compliant—eager to help the authorities, hopeful to be given the position of sous-chef. But I had had enough of taking sides. Suddenly I just wanted to be left alone.

"No," I answered.

His expression didn't change. He picked up a towel and wrapped it around his waist with a gravitas worthy of a Roman senator being draped in his toga.

"Get out," he said, then turned abruptly and exited through the frosted glass door.

The chef and I looked at one another. He had shrunk and looked more like a normal man of six feet or a little under. He rose and wrapped himself in his towel.

"What a shame," the chef said. "I was ready to ask for your references and have you fill in a W-9. We could have run a quick background check and made you the offer. You'd have been one of us."

I took my towel and tucked one end over the other to hold it around my soft middle.

"Thanks," I said, "for everything."

"He took it badly when you said you liked ships."

"Hasn't he ever gone on a cruise?" I asked, trying to remember where I left my clothes. I wanted to leave as soon as

I could, but I'd need my clothes. I tried to recall what I'd put on that morning, but I couldn't.

"I don't hate ships all that much, but I had to put on a good show for him." The chef said this and stood to face me just as the man had. If anything, I looked down slightly into that dark and contemplative eye of his. He blinked and kept on looking at me. At last he seemed to have made up his mind. "If you don't find it intrusive, I'd like to make a suggestion."

"You said I would be second-in-command, but you're not in command yourself. He's in command." I pointed an accusing finger toward the door where the man had exited.

"He commands the complex, but I command the kitchen. Anyway, may I make a suggestion?"

"Sure, and then tell me where my clothes are." I realized the room had cooled despite the mists that still hung in the air.

"You must never reveal me as the source of this information. It would be," he paused, his eye fixed on me, "indelicate for me, prejudicial. Will you promise?"

"I promise." After all, whom could I tell?

"There is a shop that sells model ships. It's run by a man whom it would be worthwhile for you to meet."

"Worthwhile in what way?"

The chef smiled. "I can't say. It's just a feeling I have. Maybe you'll even get a ship for yourself. If anyone asks how you found the shop, just say you discovered it on the Internet. Don't mention me. Will you do that?"

"Maybe."

"Do it as an adventure, for fun. What do you say?"

"Okay, I'll go."

"Let me tell you where to find it." He came forward and whispered in my ear. Although my body had cooled and I felt better, the heat had affected my senses. The air from his lips touched my ear, but instead of words I heard modulations of a high-pitched tone. I don't know how to describe it better, but it possessed a beauty that I opened to and let enter me. As the tone vibrated in my ear, my spine began to vibrate in sympathy until an intense pleasure flowed up into the chamber of my skull. When the chef stepped back, I heard the skin of his feet brushing on the tiles of the damp floor.

"But where is it?" I asked.

He studied me.

"Are you always so literal?" he finally asked.

"I didn't hear—that's all."

"I'm going to ask you a riddle."

"I don't like riddles."

"In any case, I don't want you to give me an answer. If you want the key to a riddle, just think of a recipe with a missing ingredient. That's the mystery of it. If you think you know the answer, don't be so certain. If you're in doubt, try to taste the answer. I'm sure that makes no sense, right?"

"Yes, you're right."

"Good. In the end, every riddle works in a similar way. It supplies what is missing. It discovers a new part and makes a whole."

"I'm not really up to it."

"As I said, I don't want you to give me an answer. It's merely something to think about."

"Then shoot away," I conceded, since he seemed determined to tell me.

"What number is even and odd—"

"That's ridiculous." I cut him off. "There is no such number."

"I'm not done yet." He looked offended. "What number is even and odd, and zero as well? If you can answer this riddle, be careful at crossroads."

"Are you kidding? I live in a city. Every intersection is a crossroads. Anyway, I'm already careful. I watch the lights. I wait my turn. I let cars go first."

"By the way," he went on, "you said on the questionnaire that you have a great sense of humor. I wouldn't quarrel with most of your answers, but I'm dubious about that one. I don't want to hurt your feelings, but I haven't seen any evidence of it."

"I'm not getting the job, so it can't make much difference."

"I'm going to have to start all over again with the interviewing process. It's an annoyance, a distraction from proper management of the kitchen. A bit of humor might smooth things over. It's so unpredictable. It might take us in any direction."

"Once," I said, "I knew a woman who looked at leaves and saw the faces of people."

"Is that funny?"

"Maybe she was crazy," I said.

"Did it amuse you at the time?"

"At the time I thought she could see the invisible. She seemed to see so much more than I did. I admired her for that. Now I think she might have been lonely, imagining people who never existed. But she saw the face of the sun and animals. No matter how long I looked, I only saw leaves, sunlit on one side, darker green on the other, clustered close like shingles on a roof, or sometimes alone and silhouetted against the blue sky and the sun-pierced white of drifting clouds."

The chef pursed his lips. "For myself, I'm sorry you didn't get the job. I would have liked to have you around. Maybe we could have been friends."

I felt an obscure sadness at his words, but I didn't know why or how to respond.

"Can you get my clothes now?"

"Follow me," he said as we stepped back into the hallway.

We entered a room next to the steam room, full of tall gray lockers. I didn't remember having been in there, but the chef opened a locker and I could see familiar clothes. I rubbed the towel back and forth on my head to dry my hair, then quickly ran it over the rest of my body. Khaki pants, a long-sleeved blue shirt with a button-down collar, beige canvas sneakers that I treasured because I had worn ones like them as a kid—quickly I slipped into my clothes.

The chef opened another locker and dressed himself completely in white: white underclothes, white pants and shirt, a long white apron, and another towering white hat. Only his boots, which looked like army issue, were black. He found a pen and wrote studiously on a small card.

"This is the address."

He meant for the shop with the model ships.

"But what is the name of the man you want me to meet? How do you know him?" I asked these questions as we walked back along the corridor decorated with the wallpaper of Venetian scenes. I wondered how the chef and his boss could tolerate these watery vistas of lagoons and canals.

"His name has changed since I knew him, and it doesn't matter anyway. He knew my father. Once, a long time ago, he and my father did something very brave—or perhaps very foolish—together. If he takes a liking to you, you'll probably hear the story."

We passed through the dining room, quiet now in the afternoon, the round tables draped with peach-colored tablecloths and the silver and crystal set in readiness for the rush of the evening meal.

Outside the front door, beneath the downward gaze of the gargoyles guarding the golden doorway, he extended his hand to me.

I gave him a firm grip, wondering what the frame would look like if he ever needed an eyeglass for his single eye. Perhaps he could wear a monocle, like a miner's light piercing ahead into the darkness.

"Good luck."

"Thanks," I replied.

"Let me know what happens," he said, as I turned away to go down the flight of wide steps leading to the boulevard.

When I heard him say that, I had a moment of outrage. After all, I had come here for a job, not empathy. I had an urge to turn both him and his boss in to the authorities. I could imagine what kind of corruption had made this organization rich enough to buy the restaurant, hotel, and casino, and how they skimmed cash off the top and ran illegal scams to line their pockets even further. No doubt they owned other resorts in other cities, even in other countries. Their influence spread like cancer, outlaw cells that cared for nothing but their own triumph.

But which authorities would I turn them in to, and for what? With my foot in midair above the next step, I felt a frisson, like the painful pleasure of a little shock, palpate my heart. Suddenly I wanted the chef to know what would become of me. I turned to wave, but he had already vanished into the interior of the complex.

3

"I wrote him a letter," the strange woman said to me. She looked in her late thirties, about my age, slender and smallish. When she spoke, she emphasized every word and her gray eyes took on a steely gleam behind her horn-rimmed glasses. "I told him exactly what I thought of him. No edits. No prisoners. Nothing left out."

I had no idea who she was or who she was talking about. In the large room around us a storm of people moved turbulently back and forth, a lot of them dressed up in tuxes and glittering gowns. They carried presents, and I had the feeling I must be at a birthday party. But for whom?

"I left the letter on the dining room table. He won't know what hit him. It'll be like going from grade school to college.

No high school in between. Or trying to speak English when you don't know a word of it. You get it?"

I nodded, wondering why she had focused on me.

"Because a marriage isn't like a date. It's not like ten years of dating. You know that, right?"

Why did she keep probing me and making me lift my head up and down in agreement? If she continued, my neck muscles would tire and my head would droop to my chest.

"In the end, I told him, everything is about expectations. What we wanted at one time. What we hoped for but didn't happen. What we hope for now. That's the truth, isn't it?"

My head nodded. I gave a sidelong glance to watch the elegantly dressed people piling gifts on a long table covered with a scarlet tablecloth. The packages had been beautifully wrapped with expensive papers and multicolored ribbons tied in elaborate knots. I wanted to ask her whose celebration this was, but she rushed ahead.

"You know why I wrote to him? Because I can't fully express myself if I speak. Or I should say he doesn't listen to me, not to the most important things. He has no ear for nuance. But he can come back to the letter as many times as he needs to. If he wants to, that is."

I didn't remember having said a word in this conversation. She could certainly speak, but she wanted to be better understood. I had the sudden fear that I might fail her in the same way he had.

"I said to him that once I dreamed of what could happen between us. How I wanted to unfold from within myself and wanted him to do the same. Only that didn't happen. I could blame myself or blame him. You think it makes any difference who's wrong?"

"In a relationship—" I started, eager to hear my own voice.

"A letter is more permanent," she interrupted, repeating herself. "A letter can be read again and again. He can think about the subtleties of what I wrote, of our life together. I told him how I had cared for him. How I had loved him. That what I wanted when we met I still want today." She placed a hand on my forearm and held it tightly. Her eyes looked intently into mine. "I want a lover. I want someone to confide in, someone to explore with, a father for my children, a life mate whose passion ignites mine as we go forward together. Do you think I'll ever have any of that with him?"

"I don't—"

"I won't," she answered herself with a twisting of her lips. "You know what I say? Remember to remember. I don't want to forget that he and I had good times together, especially at the start. I don't want to feel sad. I don't want to think of our time together as the unhappy decade, the wasted years. Much better to say that we drifted apart."

"That happens," I managed to say.

"No," she said.

"No?"

"You'd like it if I said he and I were equally guilty, equally innocent. But that's not how I feel."

She'd trapped me. I had to admire the way she had maneuvered me so I appeared to take his side against her.

"We married in our late twenties. As the years passed, I felt myself changing. I looked inside myself. Who was I? What parts of me might develop? How would I grow? But he remained the man I married. Exactly, unchangingly the same. People don't grow apart if one of them isn't growing. Then, sometime in the last year, I began to have the peculiar feeling that I had married someone much younger than myself. That I had reached the age of thirty-seven and would continue to grow older, but my husband would always be twentysomething. No matter how many years or decades would pass. If his face wrinkled and his hair turned white, he'd still be a youth. Happy with repetition—a dinner out at a nice restaurant now and again, an occasional show, the opera once a year, sex on Sunday mornings, and then the sports channel in the afternoon."

I could enjoy those same pleasures. I didn't want her to think me shallow, so I kept it to myself.

"I can't wait anymore," she said in a voice both fierce and plaintive.

"You shouldn't," I encouraged her.

She studied me as if I were a specimen exhibiting behavior impossible for its species. Resolving her momentary doubt, whatever it was, she forged ahead.

"It's not just the biological clock, although it's constantly running. Lessening the odds. I never thought he'd make me wait so long for children. His doubts, his career, his financial fears, and on and on with his reasons. Finally we tried. What do you think? Do children come from biology or love? You tell me."

"Well—"

"So we tried and tried. We try and try. Sex on a schedule, every position designed for procreation."

"No more Sunday mornings," I said sadly, wondering if they had a big-screen TV for the sports.

"Anyway, he didn't strike me as ready to father, to be a father. He kept the focus on himself, his little needs, his little life. I offered him something bigger, but he had to be the sole attraction. Can you get me a refill?"

She held up her thin-stemmed glass. I took it and started into the mass of celebrants. These people looked like athletes, young and strong. Joyful. I saw a woman in a pink satin gown hurrying toward me through the crowd.

"We didn't expect you."

I recollected an invitation I had politely declined.

"A change of plans. I hope . . ."

"It's no problem at all." She lifted herself up to kiss me on both cheeks. Her skin was smooth. She had a hint of fragrance that made me feel as if a soft breeze had come through groves of fruit trees. Plucking the glass from my hand, she waved it in the air. A waiter appeared with a tray of champagne. I took two glasses, wondering if I should go back to the strange woman or try to escape. If I furtively went to the far side of the room, she might seek me out and make a scene. That I couldn't bear.

"Thanks," I said, wanting to ask whose party this was. But I felt I should know, and I certainly didn't want to reveal my ignorance.

"I see who you're talking to," the woman in pink said, bringing her lips almost close enough to my ear to whisper. "Keep up the good work."

With that she turned and moved quickly back into the scrum of guests. I looked at the champagne bubbling in the hollow flutes of the glasses. Carefully I made my way toward the strange woman who, I now noticed, looked plain in her white blouse and gray skirt. She also looked older than almost everyone else in the room.

"You came back," she said, not sounding especially pleased. I realized that she might not have been expecting my return. In any case, she took a glass from my hand and half emptied it.

"What was I saying?"

This annoyed me. I didn't want to listen to her, but if I did listen to her, she could at least keep track of her own story.

"About sex on a schedule," I said, thinking I always listen for too long. I don't know the polite formulas, the deft excuses people use to slip away.

"Is that all you ever think about?" she demanded. "Sex? Surely I talked about other things as well."

Her accusation stung me. She gulped more champagne, and I wondered how many glasses had preceded this one.

"Schedules, biological clocks—what do you care?" she asked.

How had this conversation begun? Why had I listened to her at all? For that matter, why had the woman in pink encouraged me to continue it?

"Should I care?" I asked.

She regarded me uncertainly. Then, without answering, she continued.

"It's not just the biological clock. There's an inner clock too. I need a companion who can go beyond where he and I went. Someone who welcomes exploration, who values the new, the possible. Are you like that?"

"What do you think?"

"You mean you don't know?"

"I'd have to give it some thought."

She shook her head.

"That's what he said about the dance lessons. I bought him a gift coupon for a series. Five dances in ten lessons—fox-trot, waltz, salsa, rumba, and tango. I really looked forward to going. It was the first time in years I'd been excited about doing something with him. When I asked him to free up one night a week, he said he'd give it some thought. I asked a few times, but then I didn't ask anymore. Maybe you think it's nothing. Maybe he has two left feet, doesn't like to move, or hates lessons. But for me it was the end. I offered him a little bit of joy, a little bit of fun. He couldn't even say yes. That's when I started writing the letter."

She sounded sad.

"It might be the beginning," I stumbled. "Once he understands, he might take action, change. You never know."

She shook her head.

"Not him. It's better this way. Do you dance?" she asked, looking me up and down.

On a small stage near the table heaped high with presents, a jazz quartet had begun to play.

"No, not really."

She sighed. The story about the dance classes had taken something out of her. I liked her better this way.

"I don't need pity," she said sharply, in response to my expression.

"No, of course not."

"Certainly not from you."

I decided not to reply.

"What did you get him?" she asked after brooding for a few moments.

"It's over there," I lied, nodding my head in the direction of the laden table.

"But what is it? I mean, he has everything. It took me forever to figure out what to buy."

"It's totally useless," I answered.

"And it is . . . " She smiled to show me how she labored to pull an answer out of me.

"It's nothing, insignificant to someone like him," I said, and switched the focus to her. "What did you get him?"

"A life insurance policy. I paid the first premium."

My face must have shown disbelief and a bit of horror.

"Come on," she said, "it's his birthday, so he's a year older. I made a joke. Talk about something really useless—extra money to spend after you're dead. He'll think it's hilarious."

"He could throw a lavish wake," I said, getting into the spirit of her joke, "and invite all the people he'll never see again. But you must know him better than I do."

"I knew him from before," she said significantly.

We fell silent again. The noise of the party had risen, and I felt that our silence must be especially noticeable.

"You're not drinking your champagne," she observed at last.

This made me nervous, and I lifted the champagne glass to my lips.

"What do you think of first impressions?" she asked at last.

"It can take time to get comfortable and act like yourself. Sometimes you have to go slowly."

"But if you're looking for the right person, you can't wait too long. In my marriage, I waited way too long."

"That's a lot different from a first impression."

"If you're going to make a mistake," she said, looking at me with that intense gaze, "it's better to make it sooner. Then you move on, meet someone else. You have a lot more chances."

"It can be sad," I replied, "to be always moving from one person to another. Never giving anyone a real try."

"You know why I came over to talk with you?"

I shook my head.

"Your ears. I liked your ears. And it's been . . . interesting to talk with you. But I don't feel that you and I have the right chemistry. Maybe you'd be a nice friend, but I have a lot of friends. I'm going to say good night and do some more circulating."

She offered me her hand, but I didn't take it.

"You didn't have to do that," I said. "You hurt me."

She looked straight at me then dropped her hand.

"I don't play that game anymore," she replied, turning away. After a few steps she tossed back over her shoulder, "Enjoy the party."

I can't explain what happened next. I don't believe I drank a lot of champagne, though maybe I did. Perhaps what she said hurt me more than I realized. I woke up in a bathroom stall with my hands on the oval rim of a toilet. I vomited again and again, pulling up an evil-smelling yellow liquid from what felt like the bottom of my intestines. Eight, nine, ten purges poured out of me like the boisterous jet of a fountain. At last the convulsions in my gut stopped, and I clung exhausted to the toilet, my nostrils breathing in the nauseating scent and my eyes staring at the yellow waste as if to find meaning in this apparition.

"Are you okay in there?"

The voice roused me from my stupor. I spit a few times and reached up to flush the toilet.

"Yeah." With an effort I pulled myself to a kneeling position, the floor tiles hard on my knees.

"The Romans used to do that for fun." The man had a jovial, cultured voice. "After a few courses, they'd tickle the throat with a feather to make room for more."

I used the toilet for support to stand up. Twisting open the bolt lock, I pushed through the metal door to get to a sink. The man stood at the end of a row of half a dozen sinks. He was dressed more formally than the other people at the party. As I bent forward to cup water to my face, I glimpsed his white silk bow tie, black tailcoat, and sparkling patent leather shoes. I rinsed my mouth several times but couldn't completely rid myself of the acidic aftertaste.

"This champagne we're drinking tonight—it's lovely," he went on as he handed me a cloth hand towel to dry my face. "Moët and Chandon. I toured the caves there once, many years ago. Before his campaigns, Napoléon would visit to stock up. In fact, he stopped there before the disaster in Russia. Can you imagine the terrible retreat from Moscow, stumbling men in uniforms of rags freezing by the thousands while the emperor sips champagne in his cozy tent?"

Another wave of nausea swept through me and I bent over the sink until it passed.

"There, there." The man placed an arm around my waist to support me. "We have to get a taxi to take you home."

My legs didn't respond well as the floor shifted beneath me.

"Keep your equilibrium," my companion said.

I could hear the party, the din of overlapping voices and the cool, impervious sound of the jazz quartet. He guided me away and soon we were walking hip to hip down a short flight of steps to the street.

"Take a few aspirin before you go to bed," he advised, looming above the door of the taxi. I fumbled with the seat belt, and he leaned across me to lock it in place. Standing again, he added, "Tell the driver where you live."

I did and soon found myself sitting at my dining table. The layout of my apartment is efficient: a hallway with a coat closet, a pass-through from the kitchen to the round dining table in the living room, the master bedroom and a second bedroom on either side of the living room. In front of me, on the table, I saw a business-size envelope with my name neatly handwritten in a pale-blue ink. I recognized my wife's handwriting but lacked the volition to move my arms and reveal whatever might be inside.

I let my head sag forward to rest in my hands. My eyes looked down at the envelope. I closed them for the peace of not seeing. There are a few moments every day when a feeling like this, of wanting to be absent from wherever I am, takes me over. It may be depression, but it's quiet and calm, like a considerate guest visiting in my home. I certainly don't mind it enough to take any mood-elevating drugs.

I tried to make sense of why my wife would leave a letter for me. She'd be home eventually and could tell me whatever she wanted. She didn't make a habit of leaving me notes. In fact, she had never left me one before.

I closed my eyes briefly to contemplate how unfair the evening had been. I must have been drinking, but I had no recollection of the pleasure of my inebriation. I only remembered being sick in the toilet, and now my breath disgusted me and my dizzy head throbbed painfully.

I had a fleeting desire to turn on the television and use the remote to flip through the channels. But I would have to get up to find the remote. Anyway, sooner or later I had to read the letter. Carefully I lifted the sealed flap and pulled the thick sheets of paper from within. It began simply:

"I'm leaving. Any letter that starts that way is hard to write. Certainly this one is. When we married, we vowed to be together always, but what happened to the man I married? I feel like I'm living with someone I don't know, a stranger. Certainly not the man I promised 'to have and to hold until death do us part.'"

There was a lot more to read, but I neatly folded the letter and returned it to the envelope. Something had been wrong, but it had been elusive. I guess I ignored it and shouldn't have. But I could hardly weigh it all now. The man said to take some aspirin, but that would mean walking to the bathroom. I felt too sick to understand what her leaving meant to me. I wouldn't be able to pay the rent. That I knew, because she earned more than I did, and we had been scrupulous in apportioning our expenses. No more marriage, a cheaper apartment, maybe searching for a job that paid more. My whole life would change.

At last I rose and walked slowly to the bathroom, filled a glass of water, washed down two aspirin, and brushed my teeth. On my way back I picked up the remote from the worn brown leather couch and sat again with the letter in front of me. I clicked on the television, moving quickly from one channel to another. Whatever the show, the sound hurt my ears and I quickly turned it off.

I took the letter from the envelope again and began to read carefully through the three pages filled with her finely shaped script. It all had a familiarity, a finality. It didn't sound open to discussion or negotiation. I hadn't grown up. I would never make a good father. She couldn't waste more time hoping for me to change. She gave a few examples, including my drinking too much on our tenth anniversary and acting, as she put it, like a "frat boy." When I finished reading the letter for a second time, I knew she would never come back. Despite my throbbing head and churning stomach, I felt the loneliness of this apartment without her, of my life without her.

I heard a key turning in the lock of the door. It made no sense—she wouldn't be coming back and no one else had a key. I stood and faced the door, my hand on the wall to support me. When the door opened, I saw the strange woman who had talked so much and then dismissed me at the party.

"You got home okay."

"Yes," I answered.

She came forward.

"What happened?" I asked.

"You drank too much. Feeling better?"

"A little, but how did you get a key?"

She frowned. "What do you mean?"

"A key to the apartment."

"Do you think I'd give up the key?"

"But you never had a key."

She looked at me with disbelief.

"This is my key," she said, emphasizing every word as she had done at the party.

Suddenly the woman no longer looked strange. Like a blurred image brought into focus, I remembered her from the years we had spent together. Once I had found her beautiful and alluring. Once she had charmed and excited me. Once, I knew, I had chosen her for my wife.

"Your letter said you're leaving."

"Yes, that's right."

"If you're leaving, you should give me the key."

"I'm leaving you," she replied, "not the apartment."

"You can't be serious." I looked for an indication of humor, an uplift at the corners of her lips or a gleam in her eyes.

"Maybe you'd like to leave," she said.

"Where am I going to go?" I asked. "You know how hard it is to find an apartment, much less an affordable one."

"Would it be easier for me?"

"But if you're going, you have to go." I felt too lousy to be sentimental. First she had to go; then I could be miserable and wistfully recall the good times. "You can't leave and stay."

"There are two reasons why I can."

"Yes?"

"Like you, I have no place to go. If I leave, I know you can't afford the apartment. There's no reason why you should get the apartment anyway, but especially not if you won't be able to keep it."

"Then you're not really breaking up with me," I said.

"Yes, I am. From now on, don't make any assumptions about our relationship. I've moved your clothes into the second bedroom. Don't come into my bedroom unless I give you permission. The living room and kitchen are common areas that we'll share."

"I don't have to stay here," I blustered.

"Then you'll move out. Maybe I'll have to get a roommate, but I'll be fine."

"What's the second reason?" I asked.

"When people break up, they're always wondering, 'What if I had stayed? What if I gave it a second chance? What if I did this or that differently?' You and I won't have to wonder. I'll know where to find you. And if you have any second thoughts, any questions, I'll be right there." She pointed to the master bedroom.

"You're taking the bigger room?" I asked.

"I pay more rent than you do."

She spoke in a matter-of-fact way. I picked up the envelope, although I had no wish to read her letter again. Slowly, I walked toward my new room. I didn't have anything to say to her that I could put into words, but it felt awkward to leave in silence.

"Good night," I called over my shoulder.

"Yes," she replied, "Good night."

4

*T*he brownstone had no number and no sign for a shop. I checked the numbers of the adjacent buildings on the tree-lined sidewalk before returning to the front of the four-story building. I tried without success to peer through the oak shutters on the windows. Finally, I pushed the white button of the bell beside the door.

"Yes?" The man didn't sound welcoming.

"Do you sell model boats?"

"Yes," he replied after a pause that seemed to signal reluctance.

"May I come in?"

A chime resonated with a gentleness that made it sound distant. I stepped through the door only to stop in confusion because the walls trembled with motion. After a moment I realized that water was falling in smooth sheets over the walls of the entrance hall and into marble catch basins on the floor. It made a susurrus like ocean waves receding back into the depths. In the cool mist I smelled a tang that reminded me of wind sweeping across salt water. Recessed ceiling lights lit the way to the end of the passage, where the man opened the door to the interior of the shop.

"You want a boat."

The shopkeeper appraised me with eyes of pale blue that peered intently from beneath extravagant white eyebrows. A thin, tall man with a squarish face and a full head of long white hair, he might have been eighty or more, but he stood straight behind the counter and spoke with a faint accent that I couldn't quite place.

"Yes, that's right."

"How did you find the shop?"

"On the Internet."

He frowned and shook his head. "Impossible."

"But this shop sells model boats."

"I'm not on the Internet. The shop can't be found that way."

I shrugged, ill at ease.

"Why not?"

"Because it doesn't exist in the same way as other shops."

Only a single beam of light fell from the ceiling to illuminate the counter. The rest of the room remained in darkness.

"How many ways can there be?" I finally stammered.

He scrutinized me. "This shop, if you want to call it that, is not about profits or losses. In that sense it has little in common with other shops."

"If it doesn't make a profit," I said, smiling in spite of a desire to be respectful to such an old eccentric, "it can't survive."

"Ah." He nodded at this.

"Isn't that right?" I insisted. "Every business is on the Internet. That's how people know about companies—by visiting websites, not offices or factories. You must have a website."

"I don't think I'll be able to help you," he said with a wave of his hand that dismissed me.

I had been seized by a fantasy that I could make money for him. If he listened to me, he would understand how to improve the performance of his shop. My marketing savvy could quickly build his bottom line. That he cared nothing for this and wanted me to leave alarmed me and made me feel useless.

"Don't you sell model boats?"

"I'm afraid you'll have to go."

"But . . . "

"Unless you want to tell me the truth."

I didn't have a glib answer.

"How did you find me?"

I stirred myself to speak. "I don't remember."

"Liar!" The blue eyes blazed and his clenched fists banged the white surface of the counter. "I'll give you one more chance."

It would have been simple enough to walk out of this darkened room and never lay eyes on the old man again. I swayed from foot to foot, side to side.

"I can't tell you."

"You mean you won't."

"I can't," I said, shaking my head.

"You're protecting someone."

I nodded, certain he would throw me out.

"You made a promise," he surmised.

"Yes."

"And you intend to keep it?"

"Yes," I said quietly.

"You didn't find me on the Internet."

"No," I admitted, "I didn't."

"The person you promised—do you know him well?"

"Hardly at all."

"Why did he want you to come here?"

"I mentioned a ship. He didn't like ships—or, really, his boss didn't like ships. Or water. He kept talking about fire."

"What about fire?"

"Fire brings out what is elemental. It's the great engine of change."

To my surprise, he smiled.

"Do you believe that?"

"I have no idea," I answered.

"Of course you don't," he said more gently. "But why were you sent here?"

"The one interviewing me—"

"Interviewing?" He cut me off. "Why?"

"For the job."

"What kind of job?"

"As an assistant." I left out the specifics, feeling I had already said too much.

He nodded.

"He thought I should meet you. Perhaps to get a model boat. I don't know why."

The shop owner reached back to the wall and flicked several switches that turned on small spotlights in the ceiling. Now I saw the models, two dozen or so, each resting on a white pedestal as if floating in the light from above.

"Look around. Let me know if you have any questions." He began studying diagrams on the counter.

I wandered among the boats, feeling surprised that he hadn't thrown me out of the shop. I couldn't be certain what had changed his attitude. Slowly the details of the models began to impress me. I bent closer to study the care lavished on the sewing of the sails, the rigging, the decks, the hulls, the miniature anchors, and the tiny crewmen. Nameplates with brief explanations about the type of vessel helped me distinguish barks, windjammers, frigates, junks, brigantines, catamarans, dhows, galleons, schooners, prams, ketches, and more.

"Do you make the models?" I finally asked.

"Yes, I make each model," he replied.

"How long has the shop been here?"

He came from behind the counter and joined me in the display area.

"I first imagined this almost fifty years ago. But I had to travel a great deal. And I had to gather resources. The building I purchased nearly thirty years ago. A lot of work has gone into it since then."

"It feels like a museum." I admired the care and skill he had lavished on the models and the design of the shop. "I didn't see a sign outside. How does anyone know you're here?"

"People do find us," he answered, stressing the verb.

"You like sailboats best."

"I enjoy boats with sails, it's true."

"They're so well crafted."

He lowered his eyes at my praise.

"There are no prices," I went on. "How do you sell them?"

"If the right customer comes, we agree on a price."

How could he run a successful store with this approach? I wondered about the soundness of his mind, but I quickly calculated that he had purchased the building when New York City was on the brink of bankruptcy. He probably bought it for next to nothing. If he also invested in other real estate at that time, he would certainly be a wealthy man today. So this shop might be more a hobby than a business. But why had he wanted to create a shop like this? How had he developed the skills to make the models? They seemed almost to move through the space.

"Could you give me the range of prices? I mean, which boat costs least and which costs the most?"

Those blue eyes studied me like a puzzle to be solved.

"No, I couldn't," he finally replied.

"It's just hard to shop if you have no idea—"

Waving his hand, he cut me off. "Which of the ships excites you the most? Which ship could carry you across the boundaries of the known world and take you to foreign lands? What adventures might you have in those latitudes and longitudes?"

This struck me as overly dramatic, and a bit intrusive. Why talk about boundaries and foreign lands?

"I'd have to look some more."

"Take your time."

I walked even more slowly among the models. I couldn't say one appealed to me more than the others. I liked the curve of the hulls on some, and the wind-filled shape of the sails on others.

"I don't know," I said to him at last.

"I'm not surprised," he said, coming to join me again. "After all, what is the source of attraction? Isn't it concealed within us, waiting for the moment of its discovery? You can look at boats, but understanding what makes you desire one thing or another is more elusive."

"I'm not sure I understand."

"You may need more time. Don't feel any urgency. Come back on another day and spend another hour. Keep coming back until the faintest hint is amplified. Suddenly you'll want this boat or that one," he said, pointing first to the windjammer and then to the schooner.

"Yes," I said, wondering if I understood him. "I'll have to come back."

He turned off the lights, except for the single beam that lit the counter and its diagrams.

"Let me show you out." He led me into the hallway filled with the calming sound of falling water.

"Are you still looking for a job?" he asked as I stepped onto the sidewalk.

"Yes."

"I'm looking for an assistant," he said as he closed the door. "If you're interested, come at the same time in a week. I'll have something to show you."

"I love you," I said to her.

"I don't want to be unkind," she replied, her voice measured, "but I have to ask you again what difference that makes?"

"How can love not make a difference?" I snapped.

"When it's a disguise for something else."

"I love you," I repeated. "Your feelings may have changed, but mine haven't. And you did love me."

"That's true."

"Why don't you love me now?"

"I've explained to you already."

"I only know you loved me and now you say you don't."

"I said I don't know."

"How can you not know?"

"Why make this harder than it has to be?" she asked, waving to get the waiter's attention.

I couldn't dismiss my certainty that she was being unfair.

"Because it's hard. At least I feel it."

"I'm not going to let you make me feel guilty."

"You're responsible for this."

"Oh, please."

"You're breaking up our marriage."

"If our marriage is breaking up, we're both responsible."

"Like a pedestrian is responsible if he gets run over by a car."

"Don't be ridiculous."

"I'm not."

"Look," she said, "I can't accuse you the way you're accusing me. You are who you are. I have nothing against you. Once I loved you. I wish I could love you still. But you don't carry your share of the burden."

"What burden?" I demanded. "Why is marriage like carrying a burden?"

"Listen to yourself," she said with a superiority that I could sense even if she tried to conceal it.

"You could listen too," I flung back at her.

"Oh." She sighed with a look of disappointment.

"I love you," I said.

"But how do you love me?" she asked. "Do you love me enough to look at who you are? Do you love me enough to take back everything you believe about me and examine it all again? Do you love me enough to see me as I am and not the way you want me to be?"

The waiter finally arrived.

"The check, please," she said.

"I love you enough to know what we're losing," I answered, feeling the limit on my time with her. "It was so good for us. Why would you give that up?"

She put a credit card on the bill and waved away the card I'd pulled from my pocket.

"We're not getting anywhere."

She spoke the words sadly. I started to cry, the tears flowing from the corners of my eyes. I cried because I had disappointed her and I wanted her to come back to me. But I was beginning to understand what she meant, like something just visible at the periphery of my vision. Then she too started to cry. The waiter returned and looked discreetly away while she dabbed at her tears with a napkin.

"This is pointless," she said. "It just upsets us."

She signed the slip for the credit card. The waiter picked it up and glided swiftly away.

"We can give it time," I said. "We don't have to decide anything quickly. After all, we're living in the same apartment."

"Sure." She tucked her wallet into her purse. "We can give it all the time in the world, but it won't do any good. Let's not meet like this again."

"But . . ."

"It's too painful. We just don't understand each other anymore. Let's go."

Pushing back her chair, she rose.

"Yes, let's go."

6

"Are there forms to fill out?" I asked.

The shopkeeper looked at me for a moment before shaking his head.

"Will you want references?" I had been careful to return exactly one week from the time of my first visit.

Another look, another shake of his head.

"Is there a job description?"

"No."

"An interview?"

"Not really."

"Would you like to know anything about my present position?"

He shook his head, adding, "But you could tell me your name."

I told him. He smiled and offered me his hand to shake.

"And yours?" I asked

"Pecheur."

"First name or last?" I asked.

"Either."

"You're joking."

"No, not at all," he protested.

"But that isn't your given name."

"That's true. You might say it's my chosen name."

"You don't want two names?"

"I find one adequate."

"Shall I call you Mr. Pecheur?"

"Just Pecheur is fine."

I nodded.

"Why don't you spend a little time with the models? Then I have something to show you."

He flicked on the spotlights again. The model boats sailed in the pools of brightness. Again I moved among them, attracted first to one and then another. Occasionally I glanced at Pecheur, bent over the diagrams spread on his counter. I lingered awhile in front of the junk. Its shape, and especially its sails, had an ancient and exotic feeling.

"Is that your favorite?" Pecheur asked when he came to join me.

"I don't know yet."

"Would you like to see something a bit different?"

"Sure."

"Come this way."

He led me to the back of the shop and pressed a button for the elevator. The golden door slid open, and he and I stepped into a cab barely large enough to contain us. The interior was made of the same golden metal, polished to the point where I could see my reflection. The cab didn't appear to be moving but must have been rising ever so slowly. Finally the light indicated that we had reached the second level.

The door opened onto an empty room about the size of the shop on the first floor, but no ships were on display. Rather, a low white wall extended into the room like half an ellipse. It rose up above my knees and its interior sloped to form a large basin roughly twenty feet long and fifteen feet wide. Two brown leather armchairs faced this wall. Behind them, about in the position of the counter on the first floor, were a door and a glass window that appeared to belong to some sort of control room.

"Have a seat." Pecheur gestured toward the chairs. "I'll be right back."

I sat. He entered the control room, and in a few moments the lights dimmed. When the room had gone completely dark, I heard murmuring and a warm, moist breeze gently touched my face. A globe of light brightened like the sun overhead. In front of me it revealed a miniature landscape, its flatness cut diagonally by a wide river. Beside the river I saw fruit trees and a group of tiny people dressed in clothing that looked like costumes from Ancient Egypt. A small package, a log or perhaps a basket, floated on the water's muddy surface.

Pecheur sat beside me and lightly touched my shoulder. He offered me a device that looked, with its pair of unusually long tubes, like a hybrid of binoculars and a telescope. Putting it to my eyes, I saw that the package was a basket that drifted toward the reeds at the edge of the river. I didn't understand how this scene had been created. Only a moment before, there had been nothing in this space. It couldn't be real earth and water, but I had never heard of a hologram that looked so realistic. Perhaps such an image could be created of a single person, but of an entire landscape, with a river that flowed and people who moved toward the water's edge, gesturing and pointing to the basket caught in the reeds? It struck me as impossible.

I could not be seeing this scene that unfolded before me. And yet through the unwieldy binoculars I saw a young woman wade into the water and pick up the basket. She carried it to the shore, knelt, and set it down before another woman, who gestured for the top to be opened. Within I could see a red-faced baby, perhaps three months old, a beautiful child despite the contortions that crying brought to its face. The standing woman looked at the baby for a minute or more as she spoke to the kneeling woman and the others that had gathered about. Then the kneeling woman rose, picked up the basket, and joined in a slow, single-file procession as the group departed from the riverbank.

The lights lowered until the room returned to darkness. I heard a distant breaking of waves. A chilling, wintry breeze rasped my face, rich with the scent of the sea. I shivered as the unmistakable sound of waves grew louder until the plangent push and pull seemed to be at my feet. A full moon glowed high in the darkness and cast its light on gray formations of clouds. I saw ocean unrelieved by land. How Pecheur had done this I could not imagine. I leaned forward into the bitter wind blowing from the basin and reached to touch the water, but he placed a restraining hand on my arm and I rested back in my seat. A schooner with three masts bucked and dipped on the moving surface. Using the schooner for a sense of scale, I realized the waves must be forty feet or higher. The ship faced into the wind but made no progress. At times the waves broke over the deck and only the masts were visible, but then the schooner would rise again from the depths. What had happened to the crew? I shifted the spyglasses toward the steering wheel, but it had no hands to guide it and spun aimlessly from side to side. I wondered how the boat could maintain its position, much less progress, without guidance. Despite the darkness, the ship had no running lights. Looking closely at the sails, which I had imagined secured against the violent winds, I could see that only shreds remained. Without a crew, without sails, unable to progress—this boat must be doomed. Its next landfall would be fathoms down at the ocean's bottom. What did Pecheur mean by this? I swung the scopes to the prow, but the frothing of the waves over the deck and the tossing of the ship from side to side obscured the small letters of her name.

"How do you do this?" I asked him as the moon darkened and the scene disappeared. I whispered as if there were others in the audience who might be disturbed by my voice.

"We'll talk later," he whispered in reply, his gaze intent on the scene before us.

Next a large lake appeared, beneath a sky of dark and threatening clouds. Villages were clustered here and there on the swath of green that extended from the circumference of the lake as far I could see, although its farthest shore remained beyond my sight. Above the villages towered high, bald hills with ragged channels slashed into their sides by rain. I saw many small boats dotting the lake's surface, and lifted the eyepiece for a closer look. The largest boat, perhaps twenty-five feet in length and holding more than a dozen men, led a procession of smaller boats toward its depths. On my face I felt a cool mist and the force of a rising breeze. The wind must have been far more powerful on the lake, because the waves rose higher than the boats that rocked on it like bobbins. The mariners cried out and pointed at the skies, from which torrents of rain whirled and tumbled. Lightning bolts danced among the ships.

Turning to the largest ship, I saw frantic men rousing a comrade from sleep. When this man arose, a blue light began to glow all over the boat and even in the surrounding water. I had heard of Saint Elmo's fire and imagined that this must be an oddly synchronous example of that natural phenomenon. Many men gathered about and gestured imploringly to the man. Again I wished I could hear their voices, but he spoke in a way that must have been forceful. When he had finished speaking, he raised his hand with his palm facing out and seemed to speak to the skies. Immediately the dark clouds broke apart and the sun shone down on the calming waves. The man continued to gesture forcefully to the others around him, who appeared to share my astonishment.

I had to remind myself that this scene was only an illusion. No man can stop a storm. Pecheur could create whatever stories might please him. I held to these thoughts as the boats, the lake, and the remarkable man vanished into darkness. This time the lights rose to illuminate the entire room, and the large basin opened emptily in front of me. I looked for a trace of water, rock, or earth but saw nothing except the basin's smooth sides, which seemed to be made of plexiglass.

"It's amazing," I said. "The images are miniature but appear to be real. Not like a movie or hologram."

"It's done with a sort of software."

"Software?"

"Yes, to create the images for the displays."

"Like animation?"

"Yes, something like that, but more advanced than the animation used for mass entertainment."

"The people looked so believable."

"The scopes enhance the effect of the landscape."

"In what way?" I asked.

"Two programs run simultaneously, one to create what you see with the naked eye and the other for what you see through the eyepieces."

"But I moved the viewer and saw different parts of the landscape."

"Yes, it has an orientation feature."

"If I had been nearer, I'm sure I would have heard their voices."

Pecheur smiled. "I'm working on that."

"And if I touched the water, I'm sure my fingers would have been wet."

He looked pleased.

"How can you change scenes so quickly?"

"It's simply opening another file. I'd already programmed the sequence."

The conversation continued in this vein. His explanations did nothing to dispel my sense of awe. I knew so little about engineering, animation, and software that his use of them struck me as magical.

"What would your assistant do?" I asked after we had chatted for a while.

"Help me with the different projects. Handle some of the details. Take care of keeping certain records. There might be some traveling."

I had the dismal feeling that I wouldn't be competent to help him with his projects, so I didn't ask any more questions about the position. We rode the elevator to the ground floor in silence. I found myself relieved to see the familiar display of models.

"Are you ready to choose today?" he asked.

"Not today." I doubted I could afford any of the boats in his shop. Of course, I had no idea what the boats cost, but I didn't want to embarrass myself by choosing and not being able to pay.

"On your next visit, then," he offered, returning to his position behind the counter.

"What is the name of this shop?" I asked, coming to the counter and peering at the plans spread in front of him.

"The Floating World."

"I've read about the floating world, but it's about illicit pleasure."

"It comes by night and vanishes by day," he said with a smile.

"Surely that isn't what you meant."

"Must it mean one thing or another? Of course, each boat is a floating world, complete in itself. But what of the desire that comes and goes? That's what made me want to have a shop, to build the models. It made me an amateur . . . "

"Hardly," I demurred.

"By which," he went on strongly with one hand raised, "I mean a person who does what he loves. *Amator*. Not a paid specialist, but a hobbyist following his pleasures, floating first with one desire and then another, building one model and then a roomful of models. What is like that in your life?"

"At the moment," I replied, "nothing."

"Yet you came here. What can a model boat be but a hobby?" I didn't answer him.

"There's still more to see," he said at the front door.

"More?"

"I hope you'll come for another visit." Those bright, searching blue eyes looked into me. "Say a week from today."

"Yes," I agreed, shaking his outstretched hand, "I'll see you then."

7

"Would you go to your bedroom?"

"If you want to date while we're married," I answered with annoyance, "at least meet outside the apartment."

"He'll be here any minute. I'd rather he didn't see you."

"I'd rather not see him either."

"Can't you be a little bit considerate?"

"You could be considerate too."

"Do you want to pretend I'm not dating?"

"I just don't want to witness your new romances."

"Maybe you should look for your own apartment," she shot back.

The doorbell interrupted us.

"Will you get out of here?"

I shook my head and sank into the couch with a feeling of being immovable. She looked at me with loathing, then turned and hurried to the door. She greeted him with a kiss and whispered a few sentences that I knew had to be about me. He came into the living room with her beside him.

"So you're the roommate." He had a melodic voice.

"The husband-roommate," I corrected him.

"We're living separately," she interjected.

"Separate bedrooms," I agreed.

"Nice to meet you."

He extended his hand toward me. Without thinking, I rose to my feet and shook his hand. He stood a few inches above me, so I had to tilt my head slightly to look up into his green-gray eyes. He had smooth skin and luxuriant blond hair. He had to be at least ten years younger than my wife, closer to the age that we had been when we married.

"It's a nice apartment," he said, moving his gaze over the art and oversized leather couch and chairs.

"Would you like a beer?" I offered.

She looked at me with a wondrous combination of fury, disbelief, and impatience.

"Enough!" She stepped forward. "We have to get going."

"Some other time," I said.

She took him by the arm and moved toward the front door.

"See you later," he replied over his shoulder.

"Enjoy the evening," I called in return.

8

"You're trespassing," I said. "This is my land."

The dachshund stood at the center of my backyard and, instead of looking to the left or right or behind to see how he'd strayed, studied me as if I might be the problem.

"Are you sure?" he countered.

I threw up my hands to show how obvious my point was.

"But are you sure?" The dachshund ignored my tossed-up hands.

"The fence is the boundary." I pointed for emphasis to my neighbor's white picket fence. It stopped at the trunk of an enormous oak tree, after which the land fell off, from one plateau to another. The dachshund had simply gone to the far side of the tree, walked through a patch of orange lilies, and planted himself on the lawn in front of me. "And when the fence stops at the oak," I explained, "the boundary continues in a straight line to the center of the stream."

"Do you mind if I sit?"

He was so, I don't know what—polite, solemn, maybe "entitled" is the best word—that I found it difficult to say no to him.

"Go right ahead, but it doesn't change anything."

He settled himself on his haunches and opened his mouth very wide, in a yawn that let me see the pink of his crafty tongue.

"The boundary line goes right through the earth. Down to China or New Zealand or somewhere. And up in the air, cutting the clouds in sections and touching the moon. Is that what you're telling me?"

"You're playing with my words," I replied. "It's a simple boundary line. Right there."

"And it runs through the middle of the stream."

"Right."

"What if the stream shifts its course?"

I knew that, indeed, over the years the stream had shifted in its bed like an uneasy sleeper. The incessant flow, and occasional storms, had washed out at least ten feet of the far bank, across from our patio.

"Confusing, isn't it?" offered the dachshund.

"The boundary follows the surface of the ground." I said, returning to this earlier point. "It doesn't go down and it doesn't go up."

"You concede, in that case," said the dachshund, "that valuable veins of ore or any undiscovered pockets of gas or oil that may reside below your land are not yours. And the same is true of air rights."

"I'm not conceding anything. If you know so much, you know you can't just cross a boundary line without consequences. What are air rights anyway? Who can own the air?"

"Who indeed?" he replied.

"Why are you here?" I asked him.

"What is your name?" he asked.

I had a shock, because the moment he asked I realized that I had forgotten my name. Certainly I had a name. Or at least I thought I did. I could almost bring it to my lips, but it had vanished from my mind.

"How old are you?" he asked when I made no reply.

I couldn't tell him.

"Where do you live?"

Mute, I pointed to the house, with its brown painted wood siding and picture window facing toward the backyard and the stream.

"Are you sure?"

Suddenly I wasn't sure. But, then, how could I have called him a trespasser?

"Where are you from?" I asked to shift the conversation in his direction.

"The dachshund is a German dog. We were bred to hunt badgers. *Dachs* means 'badger' and *Hund* means 'dog.' Being shaped as we are, we can pursue badgers above ground or below."

"You, where are *you* from?"

He looked at me with his intelligent eyes. Instead of answering, he stretched for a long time, front legs extended so his paws clawed the grass and his rump lifted in the air. Then he rose, and without even a parting word trotted off toward the boundary he had violated a short while before.

"You're not going?" I called after him, but he had turned his rear in my direction and continued toward the spot where I had first seen him. There the tiny figure, standing on all fours beside the trunk of that giant oak, turned his long nose like a compass needle in my direction.

"I've brought the lawsuit against you," he said, "for your own good."

"What? What are you saying?"

He delivered this message and vanished among the bushes and flowers in my neighbor's backyard, leaving me to call futilely after him. What lawsuit had he brought? How could any lawsuit possibly be for my own good? It alarmed me and made no sense. What had I done to deserve a lawsuit?

"Crazy dog!" I yelled, walking across the patio and stepping down to the stream to try to get a glimpse of him.

What upset me was that he hadn't, in fact, seemed crazy at all. If he said he'd brought a lawsuit against me, he'd probably done just that. The thought of it made me miserable. The wasted time to prepare my defense, the slow wending of the case through the courts, the outcome that, even if I succeeded, would never return to me the painful hours of preparation and years passed in uncertainty. And, of course, I might lose. What then? And what accusation had he brought against me?

I didn't know the answers to these questions. And many others, it seemed. Kneeling to dip my hand beneath the stream's surface, I felt the cool wetness on my fingers and watched the ripples moving away from the disturbance I'd created. Where had the dachshund gone? I could see his dark, inquisitive eyes studying me. The ripples vanished and the surface looked smooth, but I could feel the faint pulse of the current against my hand.

9

The white-robed elders knelt before me and pleaded for protection from the pirates who preyed on coastal shipping and raided rich towns. They promised the allegiance of their realms and bountiful trade. The pirates' forts I razed to rubble. Their ships I fell upon like a great storm that cannot be resisted. When the prisoners came in endless columns before me, I hardened my heart and fed the earth with their corpses.

From the log of Cheng Ho, admiral of the western seas, voyage of the fifth armada

"No pets are allowed," he said severely.

"I understand."

"Do you have any pets?"

"No, none at all."

He frowned at my reply.

"You don't like animals?"

"I do like animals." I had been thinking of buying a hamster for companionship but I hadn't made the final decision yet. "I'm just busy."

"Why are you looking for an apartment?"

"I thought I'd like to move."

"What's wrong with where you live now?"

"Nothing really."

"You need a change, a new neighborhood?" He spoke with a derisive tone.

"Let's say it's time . . . "

"Well, that explains it." He continued in the same unpleasant manner. "And what brings you here?"

Like a name on the tip of my tongue, I found I couldn't quite remember how I had heard about these apartments. "Didn't you advertise?"

"We don't advertise." He looked down his nose at me. He was a man about my height and age, with a bald head, gray suit, and matching vest accented by a crimson tie carefully shaped to form small pleats below the knot.

"But you are renting?"

"To the right applicant, with the right job, flawless credit, and excellent references, of course we're renting."

Suddenly I couldn't recollect whether I met those qualifications. His high standards made me feel uneasy and a bit unwanted, but I asked, "Do you have any one-bedroom apartments?"

"Aren't we getting ahead of ourselves?"

"What do you mean?"

He raised his right hand and rubbed his thumb and fingers together. Beyond the greed in his eyes, I could see he took pleasure in this. He knew I needed the apartment, and he wanted to show that he held the power. I almost turned on my heel to leave, but my right hand reached into my pocket. I didn't recall going to the cash machine, but I could feel a sheaf of paper money.

"Aren't you the owner?" I asked.

"No, just the agent." He kept rubbing his fingers, and I squeezed the wad of bills more tightly. "Hardworking and underpaid. Always doing my best for the boss but never getting what I'm worth."

"That's tough," I said.

"Keep your sympathy," he snapped. "I don't need it. A little charity will do fine."

I handed him the money.

"You said a one-bedroom?"

"Yes."

"We have many one-bedrooms. All shapes and sizes."

I thought finding my own place would be impossible, but now I had hope.

"It doesn't have to be huge," I said. "I'll be living by myself."

"No little lady for companionship?"

Even in the better mood induced by my money, he had a sneering quality. However, I kept in mind my need for his help.

"No."

"Why not?"

"I just don't."

"There must be a reason."

"What reason?" I asked. "What do you mean?"

"We have a preference for married couples. Stability, you know."

"I am married. In fact, I'm living with my wife now."

"Then why are you looking for an apartment?"

"It isn't going well." I felt diminished admitting this to him. "In fact, I think we're separating."

"You're getting the jump on her? A little surprise?"

How could someone so unpleasant have a position dealing with the public?

"That's not it. She wants me to move out."

"Ah, well. Don't look so down. You'll get over it. And it won't take a thousand years. It probably won't even take a thousand days." Here he scanned me up and down. "You look pretty needy to me. In fact, you're the kind—"

"What are you talking about?" I would have broken in sooner but I couldn't believe what he was saying.

"You're the kind," he repeated imperturbably, "that needs a little lady looking after you. You'd wilt like a flower if you had to be on your own. So I'm guessing sixty days, and then you'll take the tumble into love. Mark my words and mark your calendar. And in this building complex, you'll find a lot of enchanting, single young women. Ah, the bliss of new romance, new beginnings . . ."

"Do you rent apartments or just talk?"

Immediately he had an injured look.

"I'd appreciate an apology," he said.

"What for? You're the one who's way over the line."

"You know what for," he said.

I hesitated. Certainly I felt wronged. How could he speak to me the way he had? But, then again, I had cast aspersion on his professional skills. While I might feel only the slightest connection to my own work, he might gain tremendous satisfaction from being a rental agent and feel his self-worth bound up in whether the public found his performance exemplary. Also, if I didn't apologize, he might not show me any apartments and I'd be stuck where I was.

"I'm sorry."

"Apology accepted," he said graciously.

"But you said you prefer married couples. How can there be so many single women in the apartments?"

"If you're lucky," he said with his leering smile and a knowing wiggle of his eyebrows, "you get an apartment with a woman already in it."

"You're kidding."

"But I got your attention. I'm not easy to fool and I can see what you want. Now," he took me by the arm and led me to a wall papered with floor plans, "here is what we have to choose from. Basic shapes—choose what you like. You can start with this triangle, then trade up later on if you need more space."

He pointed to a triangle-shaped plan on the top left.

"I've never been in a three-sided room," I said. "I don't think I'd like it."

"Picky, are we? Well, you have a lot to choose from. Here's your standard square; then we move into the rectangle. Mixing and matching is perfectly possible, so the bedroom can be a parallelogram and the living room a trapezoid. You just have to choose what you like off the chart. For example, here we have a hexagon for the bedroom and a rhombus for the living room. We have regular and irregular polygons. Pentagons are quite popular, while heptagons, octagons, and nonagons suit your specialty types. If you believe, as I do, that people are defined by their surroundings, these are significant choices. You reveal yourself, your secret self," he added, "by what you choose."

"I like this," I said, pointing to an apartment with a circular bedroom and an ellipse for the living room.

"Oh no." He shook his head. "That's not for you."

"You just told me to choose. This is the one I want."

He frowned and caught the inside of his lower lip between his teeth for a moment.

"It simply isn't you," he said. "Trust me."

"Can I at least see it and decide for myself?"

He considered this for ten seconds or so, then answered, "No."

"No?" I echoed with disbelief.

"It wouldn't be for the best."

"What kind of agent are you?" I asked. "If I'm willing to rent an apartment, you have to show it to me. This isn't your complex. It belongs to your boss. You have responsibilities you can't just ignore. Now, I want to see that apartment."

He thought again but for a briefer period.

"I've reconsidered," he finally said, "and my answer remains no."

Perplexed, I raised my right hand and rubbed my fingers together as he had done. "You want more?" I asked.

"I don't recall," he said with a supercilious tone, "that I asked you for anything."

"Then what is it?"

"These shapes are not without significance. If I were you, I wouldn't choose the circle."

"But I am choosing it."

"You're not ready for it—that's what I'm trying to say."

"Why am I not ready for it?"

He shrugged. "You simply aren't."

"How do you know?"

"I know."

"Give me a reason."

"Just one reason?" he countered. "Because I could give you more than one."

"Start with one."

"If you were truly ready, you'd understand why I'm saying no to you today. You wouldn't be pushing me to let you go in a direction that won't work out."

"You know so much." I couldn't hold back my annoyance. "Especially considering you don't know me at all."

"Have it the way you like it," he responded, "but choose another apartment."

"Why don't you choose one for me," I said, "since you're the expert?"

"I have one in mind. Come, follow me."

We left his office and went to the end of a long hallway, where stairs with ornate metal banisters spiraled downward. He descended at a brisk trot, and I did my best to keep up. The charm of the well-appointed hallway of the main floor, with its carpeting, golden-framed portraits, grandfather clock, and antique benches, vanished in the sub-basement hallway we stepped into. He slowed, under the white glare of fluorescent ceiling lights, to check the door numbers. Everything—the walls, the doors, the ceiling, and the cement floor—had been painted a glossy yellowish white. Or perhaps it was white and had yellowed, but the effect was to make my guide look sallow and nearly ill. I must have looked the same way, but without a mirror, I couldn't tell for sure.

"Here it is."

He stopped in front of a door, pulled out a ring thickly covered with keys, and began to sort through them. At last he found the right one, slipped it into the lock, and opened the door. Inside he pressed a light switch, and long tubes of fluorescent lights flickered to life in the ceiling above us.

I looked around in amazement. We stood inside a square, golden cage that I could have crossed with four strides. The bars on its walls and ceiling were about four inches apart. Outside the cage I could only see a cement floor stretching away into the distance until the light faded.

"What is this?"

"A deluxe studio," he answered.

"I asked for a one-bedroom." I couldn't think of what else to say.

"This would be easier on the budget."

"But . . . "

"Much less of a financial strain."

"It doesn't have windows."

"It doesn't need windows," he answered, gesturing to the bare cement floor beyond the bars. "After all, there's nothing to see."

"But I like seeing something," I said, "even if it's just the brick wall of another building."

He winced. "You settle for so little. This cage has bars of eighteen-karat gold. Can you imagine what it cost to build? Who among your friends or coworkers has a home that could ransom a rajah?"

"It doesn't have a kitchen."

"Let's be honest here. When was the last time you cooked?"

I had a recollection of a cooking class, but when had I taken it? As for cooking for my wife, I hadn't. Why did I feel his remark to be a criticism?

"I'm quite a good cook."

"Just out of practice?"

"What do you care?"

I could see by his expression that I had injured his feelings again.

"This is a very unusual apartment," he said frostily, "very desirable for a certain discreet and influential clientele. If you're not to be counted in that group, I understand."

"And it has no bathroom," I added.

He greeted this with a sharp intake of breath.

"Why are you focused on details?" he asked. "Can't you see the larger picture here? Who in this world lives in a room of gold? Who? Answer me that."

"Nobody," I admitted grudgingly, "at least nobody I know."

"Exactly. Everything is mass-produced, from McMansions to those boxy apartments with sheetrock walls and ceilings, cheap plumbing fixtures, and even cheaper kitchen appliances. You could rise above all that. Your home could be unique. You could be unique."

"But I don't like this apartment," I said.

"What is your problem?" he asked.

"My," I lingered on the word, "problem is that this is a prison cell."

"No no no!" He shook his head for emphasis. "We live in a world of savagery and danger. At any moment, in the most chance encounter, our lives and everything we value may be taken from us. These bars hold that savagery at bay. They ensure that your life, as long as you remain in the safety of these four walls, is undisturbed. Once you have lived here, I can assure you, you will never want to live in an ordinary dwelling again."

The cement floor trembled beneath my feet.

"Does the subway run under here?" I asked.

"No."

"What is that vibration?"

"The construction of the building is continuing. It's nothing to worry about. There won't be any vibrations when they've finished."

"They're building down?"

"Yes, but if you commit now you can definitely have this apartment, which is near the top of the underground levels. Practically the penthouse, so to speak."

"Nobody builds down," I said. "That's impossible. I've seen how skyscrapers are constructed. First they excavate for the foundation, and then everything goes up. You can't put in the foundation and then go down."

"In an ordinary building that would be true, but this isn't an ordinary building."

"What you're telling me can't be done."

"My firm has discovered certain building techniques. You might call them more modern. I can absolutely say these techniques are not widely known. However, we are able to go down in the same way that a skyscraper rises up. Think of that! Buildings of fifty or one hundred stories that don't pierce the skyline or block out sunlight from the streets and parks. Above our buildings the landscape can appear natural and undisturbed, while beneath the earth are communities of tens of thousands of people."

"But I want a one-bedroom apartment. Can't you at least show me that?"

"Ah." He sighed and shook his head. "I've tried to be delicate and consider your feelings. I've steered you in the direction of what would be practical for you. Now I have to be candid. We run a credit check on all prospective tenants. Your credit isn't exactly stellar. In fact, you would barely qualify for any of our apartments if it wasn't for your charitable inclinations." Here he rubbed his thumb and fingers together. "I'm showing you what you can afford. If I let you look at a one-bedroom, of course you'll love it. But I couldn't in good conscience rent it to you. You'd just end up further in debt, more than likely my employers wouldn't get all the rent, and I'd be in a tight spot for having shown you any apartments at all. Believe me, this apartment is the best I can do for you."

I did believe him. Even as he waited for me to speak, my thoughts wandered to a recent visit I had made to the pet store. There had been so much life there—all kinds of colorful fish in aerated tanks, parakeets and parrots and more exotic birds with flamboyant plumage, lizards and snakes and frogs, mice and gerbils and rats, even puppies that would melt the hardest of hearts. For five or maybe ten minutes I stood in front of the cage of a little golden hamster. He took food pellets from a small dish and filled his cheek pouches until his head seemed to swell. Then he ran under a small platform. Bending down, I could see his small paws working quickly to push the food from his cheeks into the corner of the plastic base of the cage.

Several times he made this journey to gather at the dish and store his food in the hidden corner he had chosen. And each time he would stop on the way back, balancing on his hind legs with his paws in front of his chest and his dark eyes scrutinizing me. The second or third time he did this, I had the absurd idea that he wanted to speak with me. That was why he kept pausing to look at me through the bars of the cage. I brought my ear closer to hear him. But even if he did speak, how would I understand? I'd studied a couple of the Romance languages, but would Spanish or Italian help me to understand this tiny, golden-furred creature with those soulful eyes fixed on me? My sense, right or wrong, was that he wanted me to take him home. He was willing to take the risk and see how our relationship might grow and change. But I didn't want to bring him to the apartment I shared with my wife.

"So?" The agent interrupted my thoughts. "Have you made up your mind?"

I stood there quietly, wishing I liked the apartment.

"I'm not going to take it."

"I won't bother to ask why," he said, not concealing his annoyance. "I've certainly tried to be accommodating."

I followed him up several flights of stairs, to the ground level. He guided me past the uniformed doormen and the revolving door at the entrance.

"Here," he said, extending his hand, "this is yours."

I reached out and took back the cash I had given him.

"But . . ."

"No play, no pay."

His fairness made me wonder if I had misjudged him.

"You know what I'm looking for," I said, returning the wad of money to my pocket. "Please let me know if anything like that comes up."

"If it's affordable."

"It has to be," I agreed.

"Maybe on one of the lower levels."

"I'm willing to make some trade-offs."

"That's wise. The elevators will be working by then."

"You have my phone number."

"Yes," he answered. "I'll keep you in mind."

11

I arrived exactly on time for my next visit. Once again Pecheur busied himself with studying and amending the diagrams spread over the top of the counter, while I wandered among the models. And again the Chinese junk drew my attention. The proportions of its high stern and low sides struck me as unusual. Its sails looked like the wings of an exotic bird that might fly to another world.

"One of my favorites," Pecheur said when he joined me.

"It is?"

"Yes. We call it a junk, which comes from the Portuguese *junco*. That, in turn, came from the Malaysian *djong*, a mispronunciation of the Chinese word for boat, *chuan*."

I looked to see if he might be kidding me. He had alertness, a brightness, in his eyes, but nothing to suggest humor.

"There's disagreement about it too." He continued. "A scholarly colleague tells me that *jung* would be better to use than 'junk.' In Chinese it means 'river.'"

"*Jung* has a more dignified sound," I agreed.

"Or *gorl* might be best, since it's Chinese for a large boat that sails on rivers or lakes."

"Ah." I didn't know how else to respond.

"Are you ready to see more?" he asked.

I nodded.

Pecheur ushered me into the golden elevator, but this time he pushed the button for the third floor. After the slow ascent, the doors opened onto a room about the same size as those on the first and second floors. A vast maze of water, miniature in scale, filled the floor. I could see a stretch of wavy ocean, lakes, rivers, streams, canals, and reservoirs—their flow regulated by a complex of dams, dikes, locks, and gates that shaped and blocked them.

"May I?" I reached toward the water. Pecheur didn't stop me, and my fingertips brushed the cool, wet surface. I wasn't sure what to say. "What is this?" I finally asked.

Pecheur smiled at my tone. "A work in progress."

"To do what?"

"Look here." He pointed at the model. "The lowlands have been painstakingly taken back from the sea. Dikes, ever larger and stronger, allow millions of people to live in homes on land once covered by water. But there is never any certainty, no matter how strong the dikes. What if a storm is stronger? What if it breaches the dikes, floods over the banks of rivers and canals, wrecks farmlands and towns?"

"Where is this?" I asked, waving my hand toward his creation.

"This is a model, not a map."

"But it's like Holland, isn't it? Is that where you're from?"

"Yes, I grew up there."

"Why have you built it? It's so complex. Is it art or something else?"

"It could be called art, but not the kind that ends up in a gallery or museum. I'm trying to find a better way to work with the force of water."

"You mean harness its power?"

"That's part of it, but also to protect against its power to destroy. I want to find a harmony between water and land. What you see here"—he pointed to the tiny dikes—"isn't flexible enough. There must be a better way."

My confusion must have been evident, because Pecheur gestured to me to sit in one of the armchairs in the small semi-circular space next to the elevator. The panorama filled the rest of the room. I didn't see how Pecheur was able to move through it, much less build and adjust it.

"To explain this," Pecheur said, as he sat in the chair next to mine, "I have to go back to something that happened when I was a young man. I attended college for several years, but I couldn't understand the purpose of studying. The war had ended, but the suffering and devastation in Europe made a deep impression on me. What could school offer in the way of solutions or palliatives to heal our wounds and make certain we never again resorted to war? These kinds of questions consumed me. With the certainty that only young men possess, I dismissed study and academic degrees as valueless. Finally, with my parents' permission, I took a year off from school. One year stretched to three and then six. I worked as a crewman on the riverboats. It amazed me how far we could travel on the network of rivers and canals that wove through Holland, France, Germany, and beyond. As I thought more and more about this network, I began to believe that it, with its many connections, offered an answer to the questions that perplexed me. I couldn't exactly put it into words, but the smooth passage over these inland waterways soothed and comforted me.

"As I reached my middle twenties, and the war years receded, I couldn't help but wonder what I would make of my life. My father practiced medicine. I considered medical school, but I couldn't decide to return to my studies. Then came the night of February 1, 1953. Our boat docked on the Hollandse IJssel River. The crew turned in at a small hotel in the town of Nieuwerkerk aan den IJssel. This happens to be the lowest point in Holland. Much of the surrounding area was also below sea level, but the dikes holding back the sea allowed people to make their homes there. I had trouble falling asleep, because I kept wondering what would come next in my life. I felt I had to make a choice, but I didn't desire one career or another. In a way, I lived outside the everyday world, floating on the rivers and canals, waiting to discover what would become of me.

"In the early morning hours an enormous storm came in off the North Sea. A huge, spinning dome of water, much like a hurricane, hit the southwest coast of Holland at high tide. Gale-force winds pushed the surge to record heights, as much as fourteen feet. In some places, when the dikes broke, walls of water twelve feet high rushed like a flash flood through the countryside, destroying everything. In the middle of the night I heard men yelling and banging on the doors of the hotel. I pulled on my trousers and rushed into the hallway. Our captain told the crew to get their gear and assemble in the lobby. Around us, in chaos, half-dressed people were evacuating the hotel to seek higher ground.

"When we assembled, the captain introduced the mayor of the town. He came straight to the point. The tidal surge from the North Sea had blocked the flow of the river. Tremendous pressure was being exerted on the *Groenendijk*, a dike on the west bank of the river. Never reinforced with stone, the *Groenendijk* was breaking apart. If the hole could not be plugged immediately, the flooding would imperil three million people in the city of Rotterdam and the surrounding lowlands to the east. The mayor ordered our captain to take our boat and ram it into the hole in the dike. Only that, he said, might hold back the water.

"Then our captain spoke. He simply said that whether we succeeded or failed, we were all likely to die. He wouldn't want any man to go against his will. Instead, he asked for three volunteers from the crew of eight. I stepped forward without hesitation. Really, I didn't think at that moment. The captain chose among the volunteers who had neither wives nor families. Leaving our comrades behind, we hurried out into the high winds and the stinging rain that flew horizontally along the streets.

"On board the ship, I went below deck to warm the engines. There, alone, I began to doubt my choice. I was young and could have a long life. If I remained on board, I would be an accomplice in my own death. What hope could a ship, even a ship of steel, have against these forces of nature? If we didn't sink before we reached the levee, how would the ship survive the impact? Why should I die for some mad scheme that had no hope of success?

"As these thoughts ran through my mind, my hands moved over the controls, bringing fuel and fire to the hidden chambers. When the captain called on the intercom, I told him the engines were ready. The ship began to move away from its moorings.

"I knew I would die. At the same time, in that windowless hull of metal that carried me beneath the water's surface, I couldn't believe in that death. The captain called for maximum power. The pressure gauge trembled in the red zone. I could smell a burning scent in the thick odor of the fuel. We would either explode or hit the levee at full speed.

"Our captain feared that the ship might go right through the gap in the dike and fall to destruction on the far side. To prevent this, he brought the ship in at an angle in front of the growing hole. I blacked out when we hit and woke in utter darkness. Acrid smoke burned my throat and lungs. Strange as it sounds, I didn't know who I was. I had no idea what had happened. A man's voice screamed a name over the intercom.

Slowly I realized that it was my name, that he was my captain, and that I lay on the hard metal floor of a ship. He ordered me to shut down the engines. I struggled until I raised an arm and felt my way across the controls to pull down the levers. For a few moments, a silence surrounded me as the engines quieted. I could feel liquid, it had to be blood, soaking the hair on the back of my skull and running down my spine.

"The floor was fixed at an odd tilt beneath me, an equipoise that could only mean we had plugged the fissure in the levee. The ship trembled and groaned like a man tormented on a rack. I realized how temporary our achievement might be. The surging waters must be working ceaselessly to dislodge and destroy us. I could do nothing but wait and hope. But later, on the bridge with the captain, I saw that the rushing current had pressed the ship across the dike like a floodgate. By a miracle, the very force of the water had held our ship in place and saved the dike. I knew that if I lived through the storm, I wanted to harness and shape these great forces."

"Were you afraid?" I asked.

"In a way, yes." He nodded, his blue eyes focused in an inward gaze. "But in another way I forgot myself. I was no more. There was only the drama of which I was a part."

"Were you afraid because, now that you knew what you wanted, you might die before you could attempt it?"

"I didn't think like that. I simply wanted to study whatever might help prevent another disaster of this kind. Because the *Groenendijk* withstood the flood, much of South Holland was spared the devastation in Zeeland where the dikes gave way."

I couldn't help but contrast my background to his. He had been shaped by war and found his calling in an act of heroism during a natural catastrophe. I doubted that anything similar would ever happen to me.

"Immediately after the disaster," he went on, "a commission was set up to determine what had gone wrong and what must be done for the future. This led to the Delta Works, a true wonder of the modern world. It included an immense double gate to stop storm surges from entering the mouth of the Hollandse IJssel. I realized that by becoming an engineer I could contribute to these projects that might take decades to build."

"Is that a storm surge barrier?" I asked, pointing to a rounded structure that spanned one of the model's rivers.

"Yes, but I'm not satisfied with it."

"Why not?"

"Because my dream is to repeat on a far grander scale what happened that night. To use the immense force of a tsunami or hurricane to protect against the very damage it might otherwise inflict. For many years, I worked in Holland to realize this vision, then traveled to foreign countries to continue my work."

"What is that?" I pointed to a channel that led from the ocean only to turn back in the shape of a hook.

"If I could determine where a storm surge would hit first, I believe the force of that surge might be directed back toward the sea to block subsequent surges."

"Does it work?" I asked, continuing to study the panorama.

"Sometimes it works. In the model, I mean, but it would need vast improvements to ever be useful. Look, I want you to see this."

Pecheur aimed a remote toward the panorama and pressed several buttons. The waves of the sea rose higher and higher against the dikes. Then, in two places, sections of the dike slowly began to lower. One section sank first beneath the pounding water, which rushed through it and into the hook-shaped channel and sped back again toward the second section of the dike, which had by then lowered. The returning water met the inflow from the sea, and for a moment the two flows perfectly balanced one another. All was still.

"It can be done," Pecheur said with a gesture of his hand.

I nodded in reply, watching as the two walls of water held one another motionless. Then, as if the force of the flows had become unequal, the water in the channel began to seep backward, and the water from the sea started spreading over the lowlands. Pecheur tapped the buttons of the remote, and the two sections of the dike rose from their nests in the ground. More remarkably, two holes opened on either side of the channel. I couldn't see the actual holes at first but simply the spiraling downward rush of the water. Within a minute, the dike stood like a solid wall and the water had completely drained from the land.

"How do you control the openings?" I asked. "Where does the water go?"

"My plan is to store it in underground caverns."

"Does such a thing exist?" I asked as he clicked the remote and the holes gradually closed.

"Not yet," he said, pointing the remote toward a different part of the panorama to show me another feature of his creation.

"Wait," I said. "What if the channel were wider and closer to the second dike?"

He lowered his head to study the remote as his fingers played over the keys.

"Let's try it." He aimed the remote to start the sequence again. One section of the dike lowered as before. Now I noticed that the channel had indeed become wider and almost touched the base of the second section of the dike, which again lowered as the water rushed through the hook-shaped channel. Seawater poured through to meet the rushing current in the channel, but to my dismay the seawater flowed right over the shallower water in the channel and began to flood the lowlands. Pecheur used the remote to open the holes and drain away the excess as the dikes rose to form a solid wall.

"It's not just trial and error," Pecheur said. "It takes hours and hours of calculation on the computer. Even so, the best I've been able to do is what you saw before."

"What if you had a second wall behind the first wall?"

"Very expensive. And for centuries they've been building walls to hold back the sea. I want the sea to hold back itself."

"What if the openings were larger and the caverns could store more water?"

Pecheur shook his head. "The capacity of the caverns isn't limitless. To lower the sea to the level of the land would mean shifting an enormous volume of water, far more than any network of caverns could contain."

"What if the holes reached to the center of the earth?" I asked. "Then the molten core would evaporate the seawater."

Pecheur looked at me from beneath his bushy white eyebrows. I felt like a fool to have made such a suggestion. No one could drill to the center of the earth, much less funnel millions of gallons of water down such a hole.

"If you did that," he said, "you would release tremendous amounts of energy. You could harness the power, just like the early steam engines did. Of course, it couldn't be done now, but what if the downward force of the water turned turbines? Even if it didn't fall that far, it could generate huge amounts of electricity."

Pecheur had used my impractical idea as a stepping-stone to explore another possibility. I could feel myself relax.

"Do you often have people help you with your work?" I asked when the conversation reached a lull.

"No, not often."

"I'm afraid I'd make a very poor assistant."

"Why?"

"I'm not handy," I confessed. "I've never built anything, not even a model plane or boat when I was a kid. If something needs to be fixed, I take it to a repair shop. I know nothing about computers except how to turn them on and use some of the programs that are already there. I've never programmed anything on my own. I'm totally ignorant about engineering. In fact, I'd say I have no qualifications to be your assistant. Honestly, I don't know why you would want me."

Pecheur smiled at my little speech.

"You're candid," he said.

"What could I do here that would be of help to you?"

"There are things in the shop. But really it's this work that I want to see continue."

"I still haven't digested what you showed me on my last visit, much less this. How can I help with something I don't even understand?"

"I have a hunch. I've pursued my work in a certain way. Engineering seemed a reasonable choice. Maybe other skills would have been even better. You offer something different from what I have to give. Maybe you won't be able to do this work at all, or maybe you'll be better at it than I am. In any event, there will be time for me to train you."

I mulled this over as we rode down in the elevator and returned to the model boats.

"This one is based on Columbus's flagship, the *Santa Maria*," Pecheur said with a gesture of his hand. "He sought a route to the Indies and discovered America. Of course, he wasn't the first to discover America, but he had a theory that opened the way for those who would follow him."

"What theory?"

"That the winds blow from west to east in the temperate zones and from east to west in the tropics. The ships of his day had trouble sailing into the wind and tended to cling to the coasts of known continents. But if they were to sail along the coast to where they could pick up winds blowing in the right direction, he conjectured, they could go back and forth across the Atlantic with those winds behind them. Once his theory proved true, explorers began to sail on the oceans to every corner of the globe."

I looked closely at the model of the *Santa Maria*.

"I doubt if I can afford to buy a boat," I admitted when I looked up at him.

"Why don't you borrow one?" he suggested.

"Could I?"

He nodded.

"I like the junk," I said.

"Then take it."

"When do you want it back?"

His eyes searched my face before he replied.

"When you're ready to return it."

12

"You were out late."

I couldn't believe she had stayed up. She always went to bed an hour or two before me.

"What do you care?" I replied.

"And you've been drinking," she added.

"I had a few drinks. So what?"

"With anyone special?" She had kicked off her shoes and settled on the couch. Shopping bags littered the floor around her bare feet.

"Nobody special."

"Just someone."

"Someone I met there," I admitted.

"Want to sit down?" She gestured toward the other end of the couch.

"Sure." I sat, not certain I really wanted to.

She looked at me and didn't say anything.

"Taking care of some shopping?" I asked.

"You're not wearing your wedding ring."

She ignored my question and leaned forward to peer sharply into my eyes.

I felt guilty, even though she had been the one who pulled away.

"I'm not sure we're married anymore."

"I see." She didn't elaborate, but continued to study me.

"Do you want something?" I finally asked.

"Maybe."

"What is it?"

"I'm not sure you can give it to me. In fact, I'm pretty certain you can't."

"Try me."

"I saw the model boat on your desk," she said, changing the subject. "Where did it come from?"

"You were in my room?"

"You left the door open, so I looked in. I didn't touch any of your precious stuff. It's a beautiful model, but you have no interest in boats."

"A friend is lending it to me. I might be interested in a model boat. It's a new interest."

"Really?" She looked doubtful. "So a lot's going on with you."

"What do you mean?"

"I heard you've been looking for an apartment."

"How could you hear that?"

"It doesn't matter who told me ... "

"It matters to me," I said, my voice rising.

She came closer and raised a hand to touch my cheek. The familiar softness of that skin silenced me.

"I'm sorry if I've hurt you."

As usual, my anger felt like self-pity. Why didn't she love me anymore? I wouldn't be looking for an apartment if she hadn't left me. And at the first hint of intimacy I wanted to make the sort of clinging assertion that she hated and I didn't like either. She raised her lips to mine and with a simple, lingering kiss restored me to myself in a way I never could. Embarrassing to depend on another to create that inner certainty, but I did. Easily, as if it had never been in question, she rose with my hand in hers and led me to the bedroom we had shared.

I found myself in an embrace I had lost hope of ever experiencing again. We moved with a languid slowness, as if waves lifted and lowered us together. She raised herself on her arms and rocked above me. I watched through half-opened eyes like a voyeur. This feeling of being an outsider made me anxious and I rolled her beneath me. I quickened as if to join us inseparably in a frenzy of movement.

"Make love to me," she cried out.

For a moment I had the dizzying sense that my gyrations had wakened in her an insatiable need for me.

"Make love to me," she cried out again, but now the words sounded torn from her and I heard her inflection. She meant that my lovemaking failed her, that she didn't feel loved by me whatever the connection of our bodies. I tried to slow myself, but my body had its own hurried rhythm.

"Stop it." Her voice pleaded at first, then gave way to anger. "Stop it!"

What did she mean? Stop the thoughts pouring through my mind? Stop moving my flesh on hers?

She started hitting me, swinging her hands up from the sheets to slap my shoulders, my chest, my face.

"You're just screwing me. Get off. Get off me!"

I separated from her and stood beside the bed.

"Get out of my room." She curled on her side. "Leave me alone."

She didn't sob, but I could hear the whining of her breath. She clutched a pillow in her arms the way a child might hold a teddy bear. I considered sitting beside her and comforting her, but I didn't know what to say. I felt she had rendered a judgment against me. Nothing I could do would change it. I picked up my clothes and closed the door behind me. Standing in the quiet of the living room, I wondered how this could have happened. What had made her want me, however briefly? Fear that I would find an apartment of my own? But if that were true, she must have at least a small hope that we could mend our marriage. Whatever it might be, I felt I had lost an opportunity that wouldn't come again.

I locked the door to my room and sat at my desk. I looked at the model boat, the curve of its sails implying wind that moved it forward, toward some destination. My gaze fell lower, to the organ that with my wife had been puffed up and certain. Now shrunken, it burned from that unfinished connection.

It occurred to me that I could relieve the inflammation. I took hold of the wrinkled relic to give it a new life. But my touch made me think of her. Across the living room, behind a closed door, curled on the bed that had been ours. I could be with her in moments. I worked my hand more quickly, but the ruin showed no sign of aspiring to its former lofty architecture. No matter how gently or forcefully I caressed it, the small knob of flesh remained shapeless. I could feel its smallness, but it seemed to barely register the warmth and presence of my hand. A chill spread throughout my body, my spine quivered, and I wondered if it would ever rise again.

At last my focus shifted to the model on the desk in front of me. I had pushed the computer screen to one side to make room for it. Why did Pecheur trust me with such a delicate, painstakingly detailed miniature? It would be easy to label him an eccentric. After all, his life's work was to find a way to use the energy of a storm to restrain its own destructive force—to make walls of waves and winds.

I searched on the Internet for "Junk China history." Nearly eight million links came up, but I found myself absorbed by the first few sites I visited. In 1403 the warrior Chu Ti usurped the Ming Dynasty throne. Taking the advice of court eunuchs who knew of the wealth to be made from commerce, Chu Ti decided to build fleets of treasure ships and expand the reach of his empire. He appointed his most trusted commander, Cheng Ho, a Muslim, as admiral of these fleets. In 1405 an armada of 317 enormous junks, some reported to be as large as 500 feet in length and 150 feet in width, began the first of seven epic voyages that would take place over the next three decades. Traveling as far as the coasts of India, Persia, Africa, and even perhaps Australia, Cheng Ho's armadas brought trade and tribute to China.

I could feel the excitement of this epic venture that had been entrusted to Cheng Ho. His discoveries surpassed those of Columbus, who sailed almost a century later. Wanting to know more about his life, I entered "Cheng Ho biography" and turned up 213,000 links. Going to a site about Muslim heroes, I found that Cheng Ho made the hajj, or pilgrimage to Mecca. The site showed one of his ships superimposed over one of Columbus's to illustrate that the Chinese ships were four or five times larger. In fact, Cheng Ho's immense junk was portrayed as having nine masts and sails. Following a link to "Chinese Mariner Cheng Ho," I discovered that he lived from 1371 to 1435 and, in twenty-nine years, traveled thirty-five thousand miles and visited thirty countries. His tomb, in the port city of Nankin, has been restored within the last generation. A memorial hall, built in the Ming style, houses navigational maps from his journeys and pictures of him. Outside, a series of steps and stone platforms lead to his reconstructed tomb. Twenty-eight steps rise to the summit of the tomb, divided into four sections of seven, so that each step represents one of Cheng Ho's journeys to the west. On the top of the tomb is the Arabic inscription *Allahu Akbar*, "God is the Greatest."

As I considered the great adventure and danger of Cheng Ho's undertakings, I wished I had even a tiny fraction of the excitement and purpose that had been his. I had a desire to see Cheng Ho's face and searched until I found a portrait of "the admiral of the western seas," as he was known. It shows a large, handsome man dressed in an elegant, gold-embroidered white robe accented by the black of a thick belt, a flowing cape, and a tall hat. The embroidery covers his chest and abdomen and, in a separate wide band, goes around his knees. I looked for an image in the beautiful curving patterns but couldn't find one. I studied his face. To me he appeared intelligent, decisive, and powerful, his left hand resting on the hilt of a sword. However, he didn't look Chinese. The text that accompanied the portrait explained that Cheng Ho had lived in one of the last Mongol strongholds. Overrun by the resurgent Chinese armies when Cheng Ho was eleven, the captured boy had been made a servant to Chu Ti, then a Ming prince, one of the twenty-six sons of the emperor.

Reputed to stand seven feet tall, Cheng Ho possessed skills in both war and diplomacy. I discovered maps of his travels and studied the routes he sailed. On his fifth voyage, he landed in what today is Somalia and brought back a giraffe that the Chinese celebrated as a celestial unicorn. According to some sources, the Chinese might have landed in the Americas decades before Columbus if Cheng Ho's explorations had been continued by a successor. I learned that Cheng Ho was probably not buried in his tomb at Nankin. More likely he died during his seventh voyage and his burial took place at sea.

One final fact left me pondering for some time. Cheng Ho was a eunuch. He had been castrated, at the age of thirteen, along with the other young prisoners with whom he was taken, and placed in service to Chu Ti. As Chu Ti rose to become emperor, Cheng Ho rose along with him. But had the sacrifice been worth the reward? Which meant more—his freedom, his Mongol heritage, and his sexuality, or his status and achievements as the admiral of the western seas? If it had been up to Cheng Ho, which would he have chosen?

13

"Your problem," the doctor said, "isn't uncommon. Fortunately new medicines have been developed—"

"I don't want medicines," I interrupted. My anxiety about my condition made me excitable. If I had a routine complaint, such as a sore throat, I would have shown far more deference to the six diplomas hanging on the wall. "I want to get better, be normal. I've never had this happen before."

"A lot of men have it from time to time. It's part of the aging process, sometimes stress related."

"I'm not old enough," I protested.

"There is no single age when sexual function starts to diminish. It has to do with health, genes, circumstances."

"I'm not even forty."

He glanced down at my chart. I had found him through the website for my health plan at work. I chose him because his office was close by and he could squeeze me in for an appointment in two days. A tall, lanky man with thinning curls of dark hair and a long white hospital gown, he had deep-set dark eyes that looked intelligent and concerned. I couldn't understand why my condition didn't alarm him. Perhaps I should have searched for other doctors or taken more time to study his credentials.

"Let's start with the examination," he said cheerfully, rising from behind his desk and opening the door into another small room. "Then we can discuss causes and cures."

I followed him into the room, which had an examination table with some machines next to it, cabinets on the walls, a small sink, a red wastebasket with "Hazardous" emblazoned on its lid, and a rolling black-seated chair.

"Undress, please, and put on this gown." He gave me a blue gown that tied in the back. "I'll be back in a minute or two."

I shed my clothes and reached behind myself to tie the gown.

Returning, he pointed to a metal stand at the base of the table.

"Step up there," he said, pulling on translucent rubber gloves that he took from a box by the sink.

I did as he asked. I looked away as one hand moved aside the gown and the other squeezed my testicles.

"Cough, please."

I coughed. His hand shifted.

"Cough again. Good. Now stroke the penis."

Taking a firm hold on my penis, I gave half a dozen pulls from bottom to top. He studied the tip when I had finished.

"Okay. Now stand and face away from me. Place both hands on the table and lean forward."

He took a tube of lubricant from beside the sink and casually smeared a glistening, translucent glob over the middle finger of his rubber-gloved hand.

"Relax. This will only take a few seconds."

I felt his finger slip inside me. His fingertip pressed in small circles on my prostate. At last he removed his finger, handed me some tissues, and pulled off the glove, which he discarded in the red waste receptacle.

"Nothing wrong there. Of course, we'll do a PSA, but it's nice and smooth. Stand and face me," he said, pulling on a fresh glove and studying my penis again. "That's fine. Now lie back on the examination table."

I did, and he pulled out a support for my legs. He brought his chair around to the side of the table.

"This will be a little bit cold. I want to look at your bladder and kidneys."

He put lubricant on a silver probe attached by a wire to a machine and pressed the cold tip of the probe to one side of my stomach.

"Bladder looks normal," he reassured me, studying a screen on the machine. "Roll a bit toward me."

He moved the probe to my left side and then my right.

"The kidneys are healthy."

He rose.

"Lift up your feet."

I wanted to ask why, but didn't. He slid the metal support back into the table, then raised a bar from each side and placed my heels into what looked like stirrups.

"They've made tremendous strides in recent years," he said as I felt the latex gloves opening the cheeks of my buttocks and applying lubricant again. "Astounding treatments, almost beyond belief. Some are experimental, of course, but a limited number of patients are invited into the testing process."

I could feel a cold, metal object entering me. I wanted to object or question him, but his seamless patter didn't invite interruption.

"They run a risk. There's no doubt about that. Perhaps the treatment won't work. It might even have harmful side effects. But if your condition is incurable, what risk would be too great? None I can think of. Ah, just as I thought. Please hold still a little while longer. Very interesting."

I couldn't imagine what could be interesting. In a moment he withdrew the object, pulled out the support again, and took my feet out of the slings in which they had been suspended.

"Please put your clothes back on and meet me in my office. Oh, yes, and bring a urine specimen with you."

He handed me a plastic cup and left me alone.

"What do you think?" I asked when I placed the half-filled cup on the front of his desk and sat in an armchair facing him.

"It can definitely be treated," he said. "In fact, you have a variety of options."

What relief I felt!

"There are several directions we might pursue. It's a bit like a detective story. We suspect this and then that, but in the end," he smiled at me, "we always get our man."

"What do you think caused it?" I asked.

"Simply being human," he answered.

"What?" This answer caught me off guard. "But we all suffer from that. Why me and not someone else?"

"I mean that humans aren't angels."

For a moment I couldn't speak. The doctor looked perfectly sane. He spoke in a normal way. He had diplomas on his walls.

"Um . . . "

Sensing my confusion, he continued: "Angels are immortal and have no need for sexuality. An angel would never come to my office and complain about the loss of sexual function. It would be an absurdity."

"Do angels come here?" I asked.

"Only with an appointment."

I smiled dubiously at his joke.

"It's a mystery, as I said before, and a good detective explores every possibility. What seems improbable at first may lead to the solution."

"You said you have treatments. What are they?"

"I could offer you a prosthesis. I have a file here with some information." He pulled open one of the desk drawers and started searching through the papers inside.

"I don't think," I said in a chilly voice, "I want a prosthesis. I want to be normal again."

"Do no harm," he said. "That is the essence of the Hippocratic oath."

"That says nothing about curing."

"Of course, but everything else will be invasive. Even pills in their own way."

"But . . . "

"I can offer you an inflatable insert. It involves a small surgical procedure, and then you'll be able to use a remote to create erections at will."

"That's not what I want."

"I don't like it either," he agreed. "I'm against surgery if it can be avoided."

"What else?"

"I mentioned the new medicines. They're getting more and more powerful."

"I'd prefer not to use pills."

"But we're running out of options."

"There must be something else. Exercises," I offered, "or meditation?"

"No harm in that," he agreed, "but no guarantee either."

"What else?" I asked.

"There's only one remaining option. It's in the experimental stage, but I believe I could have you accepted into the program."

"I'm certainly interested. What would be involved?"

"Pregnancy. New discoveries have proven that this is not only possible but desirable. What you see as a symptom, I see as the beginning of a cure. The very fact that you can't have erections means you are ready to move beyond that stage of your life. You're ready to hold a new life that will grow within you. You can cross the boundaries that have contained you for so many years. It's only natural. We aren't meant to stay forever the same."

"I can't have babies," I protested quietly.

"Wait, let me find the articles." He began to rustle through the sedimentation of papers in his desk drawer. "It's only in the professional journals. The popular media haven't picked up the story yet."

"No!" I said forcefully. "I am not having a baby."

"Calm down," he said sharply, looking up at me. "Are you so afraid of being a pioneer? They said a sixty-three-year-old woman couldn't have babies, and now that's old news."

"But at least she was a woman."

He shrugged and asked, "What miracle is greater than birth? Think of the adventure—to be both a man and a mother. Think of the reward of holding within you something tiny, barely existing, and carrying it to term, giving it life from your life, delivering it into the world."

I shook my head. I should have left earlier, but his enthusiasm cast a spell.

"No," I said, "that's not for me."

"Too bad."

"So, what can I do?"

"You've heard all the possibilities. You have to make a choice."

"Tell me more about the pills."

His lips pursed in disappointment. "So you're determined to be the way you were before."

"Yes, that's right."

"The pills work for most men. I'll give you a strong dosage. If you have an erection that doesn't go away in, oh, four or five hours, you should give my office a call. Other side effects might include constipation, fainting, and blindness."

"Fine."

He scribbled on a prescription pad and passed the sheet to me.

"Give a call if you have any difficulties."

"Yes, thanks."

"And come back in six months for another checkup."

I rushed to the neighborhood drugstore and waited for the prescription to be filled. Once I had the plastic bottle in hand, I slipped down an aisle to escape the gaze of the pharmacist and swallowed one of the bright-orange pills. At my apartment I locked the door to my bedroom, shed my clothing, and settled into the desk chair facing my computer and the junk with its puffed sails.

Gently I rubbed my inert flesh. I wanted to keep my mind blank, free of distractions and worries. Slowly, more quickly, slowly again, my hand moved and time passed as I worked to raise this ruin to its past glories. Stray thoughts slipped into my mind. Around the globe, at every moment, there must be millions, ten of millions, making a sexual connection. And when those lovers slipped apart, others were entering or being entered, being touched and touching, in numbers beyond counting. My biceps began to burn from the repeated motion, and I looked down at my conscientious objector. What sort of mind did it have? How had it decided to take this leave of absence? Why had it refused to participate?

I stopped and gave my arm a rest. My eyes shifted to the junk, and I began to think of Cheng Ho, vaporous thoughts that rose under a pressure I could hardly describe. He'd been "cleaned" as a boy, relieved of the distractions of his sex to better serve his masters. Presumably he never made love to a woman. What would the purified Cheng Ho desire? Power? That he would have. Wealth beyond measure? That too would be his. But what of sexual desire? Had that been lost to him irrevocably? Or had Cheng Ho's sexual pleasure become diffuse, spread over all his skin, into his organs, to his bones? The blind hear with such intensity. Wouldn't the skin of a eunuch be one hundred times more susceptible to pleasure than it was before the cleaning? A simple massage might waken an ecstasy that would spread from skin to organs to bones with a joy that a normal man would never be able to know.

I protectively seized the shifting shape of my testicles in their scrotal sac. What horrid way had Cheng Ho's balls been cleaned? With a metal device considered a modern innovation at the time? Or with a sharp knife wielded . . . by whom? A sadist? A bureaucrat? A healer? Imagining being without balls made me grasp my own more tightly, but they shifted away from my fingers like mercury.

Wasn't the wind that swells the sails of the junk like the swelling of blood that fills the tube of flesh? If such a wind can send a ship from one continent to another, could it stiffen the penis of a eunuch? If not, was he not a he but a hybrid? One who had been a man and not become a woman? A eunuch could take the stiff penis of another in his slippery mouth—or his anus, buttocks slapped to engorge with blood and massaged with scented unguents to let the skinned column enter ever more deeply. Such a eunuch would be receptive, yes, entered, true, but would he have become a woman?

I stopped for a moment and stared at the ship. What if I were both man and eunuch? I would have a stiff, smooth sheath. Wanting to enter myself, I would be willing to be entered—my penis between my lips, my anus ready for my own thrust. To experience both the pleasure of receiving and the pleasure of releasing. And what of the white spurt of sperm? Sent into the beginning or end of the digestive tract, swimming toward an ovum that would be . . . where? Would the sperm end in the gastric caldron of the stomach? The endless folds of the small intestine? Or cleaned of the literal, would a sort of ectoplasmic sperm swim to the solar plexus, the heart, the missing sack of my genitals, to work the mystery of impregnation and fill me with the growing life the doctor had offered me? Well, he had gone too far. I didn't want to be a eunuch or an angel. I wanted the familiar, the safely repetitive.

Yet these odd thoughts continued to flood through me. Might cleaning leave a terrible ache like that of an amputee whose lost leg still sends signals from uprooted nerves that say, "I am here. I have never left. Place your weight on me." But in this case it wouldn't be a lost leg or a forearm but the spongy globes of my testicles that would be gone. Would the nerves sing the same way, carrying messages of pain or desire to the spine and the brain? Would my balls have a phantom life?

Then I recollected a man, a person I should say, who had the fully developed sexual organs of both a man and a woman. What sensations would such a man-woman be capable of achieving? I never knew this person, but I read his/her first-person story. He/she had no preference with respect to taking the role of man or woman, although being a woman brought presents that he/she liked. Of course there's more hermaphroditism than I ever realized growing up in a time when the norm allowed only two sexes, not modulations on a sexual spectrum. But could someone have the fully developed organs of both sexes and enjoy sex regardless of the sex of his/her partner? If this could really happen, what if it happened to me? What would it feel like to be not one sex but two, no longer a provincial from the town of man or woman but a cosmopolitan embodying both lover and beloved?

What of the ancient philosophers who speculated that man and woman had once been joined as a whole? The separation of the sexes left each of us searching for a beloved to make us complete. Would possessing both sexes oneself save a person from this search? Or did the philosophers mean that the soul is incomplete? If that's true, where would such a person search for what is missing? Or, thinking of it another way, if the quest is for a soul mate, then a eunuch would be as whole as anyone else. His ache for a partner would be the same as the soul ache of anyone else. I drifted a bit, like a reader nodding with sleep while the hand continues to turn pages. Gandhi came to mind. Not as the great liberator of India, but for an almost unknown episode that had stayed with me despite my having read of it quite a while ago. From the time of her infancy, Gandhi's granddaughter had slept with him in his bed. When she reached the age of eleven, Gandhi's advisors began to warn him against letting the girl continue to sleep with him. They feared that his political enemies would use this to injure his reputation and his effectiveness as a leader. He replied that his sexual life had long been over. In fact, he said, the flesh of his sexual organ had changed in color to gray and its composition had become viscous, nearly solid. Instead of going into the world, the energy of his organ now rose within his spine to roost in his skull. The author then went on to speak of the transforming power of this energy that twists about the spine in upward-rising spirals. Gandhi's advisors, however, persisted. Finally, despite wanting to continue this closeness with his grandchild, Gandhi agreed to sleep alone.

One disturbing aspect of the story of Cheng Ho returned to me a number of times after I first found him on the computer. In the Ming court, there were always competing factions, one favoring exploration and the other preferring isolationism. After Cheng Ho's death, an able man came forward and proposed to continue the admiral's explorations. The new emperor, influenced by his Confucian advisors, who valued tradition, decided against further expeditions. In fact, within a hundred years, overseas trade was forbidden and sailing from China in a multi-masted ship was punishable by death. How terrible to want to explore but be limited by others' fear. Who would Cheng Ho have become if he had never held the rank of admiral of the western seas and commanded his giant junks on their far-flung voyages? Would he have remained forever on the soil of China, on the shore at Nankin, looking to the sea and wondering what might have been?

Staring down at my wrinkled flesh, I didn't have to wonder what might have been. It was evident enough that the pill had failed. For a time, I might be more angel than man. I didn't want to visit that crazy doctor again, so I decided to do nothing at all. Do no harm—if ever a phrase lacked ambition . . . Surely I could aim higher! Or maybe not. Maybe it would be best not to aim. Maybe that would be best.

14

I rang the bell, heard the gentle chime, walked through the misty hallway with its shimmering waterfalls, and found myself again in the presence of the elderly model maker.

"Welcome," he said with a warmth that made me feel he had looked forward to my return.

"Hello."

"So a week has gone by," he observed, coming from behind the counter and offering me his hand.

"Yes." I felt the thinness of his palm when clasped in mine.

"Did you enjoy the boat?"

"Yes, very much." I couldn't tell him about the flood of fantasizing the boat had started in me. "I've brought it to return to you."

"You aren't buying it?"

"I feel it belongs here."

"Perhaps another boat would be better."

"No no, I don't think so. These models should be displayed for everyone to enjoy, just as you have them."

Pecheur took the package and returned to his counter, where he began unwrapping the junk. Finished, he placed it on its pedestal. We stood back and looked at how the ship filled the empty space.

"Are you still looking for an assistant?" I asked.

"Yes."

"I do want the position."

"It would mean living here. I may have forgotten to mention that."

He had forgotten, but I didn't care. I had no reason to share the apartment with my wife any longer, and I hadn't found one of my own.

"That's no problem."

"Good."

"When do you want me to start?" I asked.

"When could you start?"

I considered this. "I should give notice at my job. And at my apartment too. Maybe two or three weeks."

"That's fine. I'll have everything ready."

"So it's settled?" I asked.

"Yes, it's settled," he answered with a smile.

Only later, while passing the expensive boutiques on Madison Avenue, did I realize that I had forgotten to ask about my salary.

15

"*I*nvitation?"

I pulled out the squarish envelope that had been slipped under my door. My name had been inscribed in a flowery script suitable for weddings and debutante balls. I handed the gilt-edged vellum across the table.

"Did you RSVP?" the bear demanded.

I shook my head. I could hear music in the forest not too far away. The invitation was to the annual jamboree. It promised "a celebration of winter's end and a joyous awakening to lusty spring."

He pawed over the pages of a long list of names.

"Ah, here you are. Okay, go on through and follow the others."

"What group is sponsoring this event?" I asked.

He furrowed his thick brows.

"Who invited you?" he growled.

I had no idea why I'd received an invitation. In fact, I barely knew what spur-of-the-moment caprice had made me rush to Central Park. It might have been the word "lusty." I had been going here and there for treatments for my condition, but nothing had helped so far.

"It was under my door . . . " I began to explain as the line of waiting bears grew longer behind me.

"All right," he interrupted with a wave of his paw, "go in."

The entire park must have been taken over for the jamboree. I passed through the checkpoint and followed the crowd of bears as it flowed beneath the antique street lamps. Even on the wide paths, furry pelts and thick muscles pressed against me in the crush. An excited chatter moved with us as we struck deeper into the park.

Ahead, near the Great Lawn, I could see bears converging from several directions. Far too many to count. On a bandstand raised near the leaping light of a bonfire, a band of a dozen bears played drums, fiddles, and flutes in a jig that reverberated through the park. Around the fire a hundred or more bears danced with legs crossing forward and back and arms outstretched to clasp one anothers' shoulders. When the music quickened, the bears separated to leap and kick before coming together again. Tables were crowded with serving dishes heaped full of berries, mushrooms, acorns, and grasses. Bears with overflowing plates lined up to fill their cups from spigots in giant kegs.

Not seeing anyone I knew, I followed an impulse and leapt in among the dancers. I squeezed between a couple of bears, tossed my arms over their shoulders, and let the frenzy of the dance move my limbs. The drums seemed to connect me to the depths of the earth while the flutes lifted me to the heavens. The fiddle inspired a wildness and speed that had me jostling in and out among my giant companions. My perspiration flowed like spray from a fountain, and my body loosened with the heated movement until I imagined I had been created only for this, this endless dance that would go on and on. As if in confirmation of that feeling, the band ran one tune into the next so the flow of music never stopped. I had no idea how long the sponsor's permit allowed this party in the park, but I felt that only the rising sun could silence this music.

"Hey, remember us?"

I looked at the family with momentary incomprehension. The surge of the dancers carried me onward, and I made a full circle around the fire before reaching them again. I stepped away from the dance and tried to place this giant dark-coated bear, his large wife, and their two cubs.

"How have you been?" I asked, certain I had met them but not at all sure when or in what circumstances. We had undoubtedly been introduced, but I hadn't the faintest recollection of their names, where they lived, their unique concerns, or anything about them.

"We've been fine," said the father in his basso voice. "Frankly, it's a pleasant surprise to see you here. I wasn't expecting to."

"No," chimed in his wife.

"That's for sure," added one of the cubs in a less pleasant tone that made me wonder why they didn't expect to see me there.

"I didn't expect you either," I answered, still panting from the dance and wanting to show pleasure at our reunion.

"Why did you come?" asked the father.

"I got an invitation."

"Ah."

"I came home today and found the invitation. It must have taken a long time to be delivered, because the jamboree was, of course, tonight. I'll be moving soon, so it's a miracle it reached me at all. Anyway, I rushed out the door and came to the park."

"And you've been having a good time?" he asked dubiously.

"What could be better than dancing?"

He leaned toward his wife and whispered something into one of her upright, furry ears. She nodded in reply.

"Come on, Dad," complained the cub who had spoken before. "This is boring."

"Quiet down," the father said gruffly.

"Are you all right?" the mother asked me in a kindly tone. She put her paw on my waist to steady me.

My head had begun to feel light and my body rubbery, as if my knees might give way.

"I don't feel very well," I admitted. I looked down at my arms, surprised to find them white, furless, and spindly. Had I been sick? Why didn't I look like the throng of strong bears I could see in every direction?

"Some food might help." The father came to my other side, and the two of them walked me toward the tables.

I can't explain why I found the food unappetizing. The grass looked dry, the mushrooms uncooked and perhaps poisonous, and my teeth wouldn't be able to crack the hard shells of the acorns. Why couldn't I eat with the same gusto as everyone else? At last I put a few dark berries on my plate.

"Is that all?" asked the father with disapproval.

"He's not feeling well," said the mother. "Let's sit down and let him rest."

We settled at one of the picnic tables. What had happened to my fur? Where had my thick muscles vanished to? Why didn't I have claws? As I fed myself the berries, one at a time, I realized that I lacked the handsome snouts of my companions. Despite my horror and disgust at seeing myself in this new way, I gradually began to feel more in control of my body. Had I never looked in a mirror? How could I not know that I looked so bizarre and otherworldly?

The family ate without any concern for my appearance. They chatted amiably about the enormous turnout, good friends they hoped to run into, the beauty of the spring night, and how life is given a pleasurable intensity by contrasts. This exuberant party made him think, the father explained, of the hibernation from which he had recently awakened.

"How peaceful the long night of winter can be," he said. "In the darkness, with our daily concerns forgotten and our bodies sufficient unto themselves, the mind lets go and travels. Is it that way for you?"

I nodded to conceal my confusion. I had no recollection of hibernating. As far as I could recall, I had spent the last winter in my apartment with the rising steam banging in the radiators.

"You should take better care of yourself." He adopted a gentler tone, perhaps moved by imagining my long sleep to have been like his.

"I'm hoping to get better," I said.

"What's wrong?" asked his wife.

I couldn't bring myself to reply.

"Stop that, you two!" She spoke sharply to the cubs, who had been licking their white plates with their long tongues. "You have better manners than that."

"From what?" asked the father.

I shrugged. My embarrassment must have been evident, because he rose and gestured for me to come with him.

"Mind your mother," he ordered the cubs.

We wove our way through the throng and into the forest. I followed him on a small, twisting path until the ever-renewing music and the ceaseless roar of chatter seemed distant. He gestured for me to sit. I looked around and, seeing only tree trunks, settled on the ground, with my back supported by rough bark. He sat with his legs crossed, his head and shoulders still towering above me.

"What's troubling you?"

I hung my head. I would never admit to him or anyone that for the first time I had seen myself as strange, freakish, an eternal outsider worthy only to be despised or pitied. I didn't understand how he could accept me with such grace.

"You can tell me," he spoke gently. "You'll feel better if you get it out."

"I'm not what I used to be," I said vaguely.

"Yes?"

"I used to be better." Here I waved in the direction of my genitals.

"You're having some difficulties . . . "

"I can't get an erection." I let myself speak boldly but sensed other, more elusive losses connected to this one.

"Not even by yourself?"

"Not by myself, not with anyone. There's no point in my trying."

"What happened?"

"I don't know."

"Is that why you're here tonight?"

I nodded my head miserably. "Not the only reason, but certainly a reason. The celebration of spring, the new awakening. I hoped . . . "

"What?"

"There might be an elixir."

"Elixir?" He raised his thick brows and peered at me as if I had just come into focus.

"Yes."

"Like a magic pill?"

"Exactly. That's what I want."

"There are commercial products, of course . . . "

"I've tried them. They don't do a thing."

He put a paw to his chin. Tilting his head, he looked at me contemplatively.

"You're sure it's what you want?" he asked at last.

"Wouldn't anyone want it?"

"Probably," he agreed, "except for someone who didn't think of it as a problem."

"But it is a problem."

"What's sex anyway?" he asked.

There must have been a good retort, but I couldn't think of it.

"Energy," he answered when I failed to. "But energy can take many forms. Perhaps you need your energy for something other than sex."

"But . . . "

"Just consider it."

I did a quick mental survey of my daily activities, wondering which could be claiming the energy that had once found expression in sex. But this survey felt like the kind of questionnaire no one bothers to fill in. By and large, I didn't remember what I did during the day, or night for that matter. I remembered the envelope slipping under my door. I remembered rushing out to the jamboree. I certainly remembered that I couldn't have erections.

"I have a question," I said.

He raised his brows to show interest.

"Where do all these bears live? I've never seen one bear in Central Park, much less thousands."

"In the caves," he answered, nodding his head.

"What caves?"

"The park is full of caves."

"There would have to be thousands of caves," I protested.

"Yes, thousands, hidden from sight."

"That's impossible."

"It's a secret project."

"Whose project?"

"When the mayor was elected to his first term, he promised to end the housing shortage. He made a firm commitment to affordable housing. One of the easiest steps for him to take was to build these caves."

"You're kidding me. I would have read about it in the newspapers."

"I said it was secret."

"But . . . "

"Think about it. How many homeless bears will the public tolerate? That's one reason the mayor took it on first, before subsidized housing for the poor and the disadvantaged middle class. And there are certain practical advantages—"

"Such as?" I broke in.

"A cave is basically just the absence of something. All that's required is a large hole. You don't have to lay a foundation, put in pilings, find materials and workers to build up story after story. It's incredibly cheap. No additional services are needed—heat, gas, and electricity are irrelevant. Historic districts and the beauty of the city skyline are left undisturbed. And Central Park could easily host tens of thousands of caves."

"But are the bears happy in caves?"

"Where else would you want to be in the winter?" he asked. After waiting a moment, he went on, "Of course, there are different kinds of caves. Some are shallow, hardly more than an opening in a cleft of rock. Others penetrate a long distance but are straight and flat. Some go down almost vertically. And then there are the chambers that you come on unexpectedly, small nooks that can be perfect for curling up and large caverns with stalactites and stalagmites. Have you noticed how the shape of the cave affects your dreams?"

"No, I really haven't," I replied.

"Yes, that would be my only criticism of the mayor's building program. I find my dreams aren't as interesting now. The caves feel as if they came off an assembly line. Perfectly rounded, all about the same length, all flat or declining very gradually."

He piled absurdity on absurdity.

"I find it hard to accept," I said deliberately, "that the mayor would build caves before apartment buildings."

"You're still stuck on that?"

I didn't answer. We sat there, each lost in his own thoughts. The music and the buzz of the revelers still came through the forest. My companion had lowered his head, closed his eyes, and might well have fallen asleep. I could feel the hard bark pressing into my back. I shifted one way, then another. Suddenly he leapt to his feet.

"Come with me."

"Where?"

"I want to show you something."

He moved deeper into the forest. I followed, not complaining about his speed, the branches whipping at me in his wake, or the darkness. We must have walked for ten minutes before the rise of a rocky cliff blocked us.

"This way."

I followed and found myself in a tunnel. I call it a tunnel, not a cave, because obviously it had been built by machines. A gradual slope led downward. On the ceiling a translucent wire strip gave off a faint glow. After a few minutes, we reached a cave. The lighting ceased with the end of the tunnel, but I could make out the irregular contours where the cave began. He squatted and pointed back the way we had come.

"Now do you believe me?"

I couldn't imagine a better explanation for this tunnel to nowhere. I had to nod my head in agreement.

"I spent last winter here."

Realizing this was his home, I wondered at its emptiness.

"Will you come back?" I asked.

"I'm not sure."

"Why not?"

"At first I slept near the entrance, but I didn't enjoy my dreams. So I kept waking and moving deeper. I ended up in the real cave, the part that had always been there. Come, I'll show you."

With his rough pads and claws, he grasped my hand and led me away from the light until I could see nothing. Unlike the gradual descent of the tunnel, the gradient in the cave was steep, and I kept slipping and banging my feet against ledges and loose rocks.

"Watch your head," he warned.

I bent and groped with my free arm.

At last he guided me to a ledge of smooth stone where I could sit. I smelled a strong odor, like bales of hay but more pungent. Since I couldn't see anything, the source of the scent remained a mystery. Cool air flowed upward over my bare arms and face.

"Was this better?" I asked.

"In a way. There's a small niche right here, where I curled up to sleep. You don't hear a sound."

It was true. I couldn't hear the music anymore.

"Sometimes," he added, "I would quiet my breathing so I couldn't hear myself."

"But what about your dreams? I thought you said you enjoyed the long sleep, the chance to let your thoughts wander."

"You know what the hunger madness is like before we hibernate. At first I kept dreaming about foraging, but I couldn't find what I wanted. I didn't like those dreams, but when I moved deeper I started dreaming of strange creatures I had never seen in the forest. After a while I became troubled."

"Why?"

"I hesitate to say."

"I won't tell anyone," I said, thinking that might be his concern.

"Do you feel anything about the darkness?"

I had never experienced such absolute blackness, but I wasn't sure what he meant.

"What about it?"

"How many of us are here?" he asked.

A shiver shot up my spine. I had no idea.

"Just you and me," I answered, hoping he would agree.

"In a way, that's true."

"Why in a way? It either is or isn't true."

"It's true when I'm awake, but when I'm sleeping, I'm not sure if it's true."

"You're talking about your dreams." I wanted to clarify that in reality only he and I were present.

"Do you feel the air rising up?" he asked.

"Yes."

"A few feet in front of you is a deep shaft. It goes straight down. I have no idea how far, but the air rising from it suggests it connects to other caves."

Immediately I felt afraid—think how easily I could have fallen into an unseen shaft.

"When I moved this far into the cave, I began to have a series of dreams. One night I found myself climbing down the shaft . . . "

"In your dream?"

"Yes. A glow lit it inside and stone steps had been chiseled in a spiral that I thought would go on forever."

"Did you get to the bottom?"

"Not in that dream, no. But in dream after dream I returned to the shaft and climbed farther down. Finally, after I don't know how many dreams, I reached the bottom. I saw a deep stream flowing swiftly through boulders. All around was a forest that, as far as I could tell, had never been touched by an ax or a backhoe. This virgin world attracted me, except for one thing."

"What was that?"

"Nothing lived there."

"Then you were safe. Nothing threatened you."

"But I came into that world like a germ, an infection. Not just my beating heart and the pump of my blood, but my thoughts—especially my thoughts. They radiated from me. I couldn't stop thinking. I couldn't hold my thoughts back. They entered there like a vibration that would go on and on. They are vibrating there still, growing fainter and fainter but never vanishing."

"It was a dream," I protested.

"What do you mean by that?" he asked.

"If we had a flashlight, we could look down the shaft and see that there are no steps."

"And another thing," he said in the darkness, "I felt that these dreams came from the shaft. They rose like the air from that other world."

"But that makes no sense. If no one lives in that other world, how could anyone be dreaming?"

"Anyway, after that idea occurred to me, when I looked in the stream I saw I was wrong. There was life there. Enormous white fish were swimming at the bottom. They had large round mouths for sucking nutrients from the debris on the streambed. I could see down through the water thirty or forty feet. In fact, I walked on the water above them. The fish had to be as long as I am tall. Slowly they began to rise toward me. This frightened me, and when one of them came close enough, I gave it a hard kick to make it keep away."

"Did it bite you?"

"I'm not sure these fish had teeth. No, it didn't, but it began to change shape. It grew two legs and two arms. So did the other fish. I don't know what to call them, because soon they stood upright. They had heads but no faces—just white, unshapen skin."

"Did they walk on the water too?" I asked.

"I'm not sure. I think they did. I moved away, but one of them gestured as if to speak. But it had no mouth. I wanted to get away. I must have run."

"Did they follow you?"

"Not in the dream, because I woke up. But I think they did follow me, because I keep thinking about them. How could a fish change shape like that? Why would it want to? What would it have said to me? I regret now that I didn't overcome my fear and listen."

"What could they have told you?" I asked.

"You have no idea?"

"No, how could I?"

"That these are not my dreams," he said.

"But you dreamed them."

"Nonetheless, that's what I believe they would have said. I've thought about it quite a bit. And if they weren't my dreams, whose dreams were they?"

I had no answer.

"Perhaps the dreams were theirs," he finally went on. "I considered that. Now, this is all just a lot of flimsy intuition and conjecture—I could certainly be wrong—but I don't think they were the dreamers. I think they wanted something else."

"To inhabit the world you discovered?"

"They'll do that, of course, but I felt they wanted to find the spiral steps leading upward. That they wanted to climb up and enter our world. They're still evolving. Who knows what they will look like when that's finished? They may already be here."

I didn't like this idea at all. It brought to mind the world I knew—the skyscrapers rising from streets thronged with people. You could tell just by looking that they had come from around the globe, spoke a babel of languages, and prayed to innumerable gods, but not one of them, to my knowledge, had risen from a dream world.

"If they are," I said, "nothing has changed."

"Nothing that we're aware of yet," he answered.

The cave had grown colder. Or at least it felt colder to me.

"I'd like to go back," I said, half expecting him to refuse to take me. I heard the scrape of his claws on the stone; then his paw touched me in the dark. Again he took my hand. I welcomed this contact and overcame my fear of falling into a shaft. Protecting my face with my free arm, I made the slow journey toward the surface. What a relief to see the faint light in the tunnel!

At last we stood outside his den. The full moon had been rising when we entered, but now it had flown to the far rim of the sky. The stars gleamed like points waiting to be connected on a blueprint for some unimaginable invention. We walked without speaking.

"I don't hear the music," I said at last.

He stopped by the low wall of a large fountain, its winged statue silhouetted in the moonlight.

"I thought about who the dreams must belong to," he said, continuing our conversation from the cave.

"It doesn't really matter," I replied. "Shouldn't you find your wife and children?"

"No, they don't need me."

This surprised me and I responded sympathetically. "That's too bad."

He laughed, a growling catching of breath in that large throat.

"It isn't too bad. I spend my time alone because I want to. It's my nature. Anyway, I spent a lot of time imagining who the dreams might belong to. Finally, I thought of you."

"Me?" Nothing could be more alien to me than those dreams with their weird, changeable creatures. "No, that's ridiculous."

He shrugged, a great hulk of darkness.

"In any case," he said, "that's why I put the invitation under your door."

"You did that?"

He nodded.

I wasn't sure how to respond, but I decided to be gracious.

"Thanks. It was good to see you again."

"About the dreams," he said, "let me know if anything occurs to you."

"Sure, I will."

He raised a paw in a gesture of farewell. For a moment, as large as he was, he looked indecisive, hesitant. He started walking away, then turned with an afterthought.

"Good luck."

I raised my hand and called back to him.

"You too."

Ignoring the long flights of steps, he slipped over a metal fence and fell to all fours as he climbed a steep embankment. I could barely see his shape as he vanished among the tree trunks.

I sat on the low wall and watched the growing light bathe the angel who had alighted atop the fountain. One of her arms carried a cornucopia or a bouquet, I couldn't quite make out which, and the other pointed ahead of her as if to mark a direction. I knew I should go home, shower, and ready myself for the day. But as I started to leave, an impulse seized me. I reached in my pocket and brought out a handful of change. With an underhand toss, I seeded the shallow waters with my coins. Then I watched, waiting for what might rise to the surface.

16

After the exchange of ritual gifts, I asked the king why every woman was pregnant except for the very young and very old. He swore that a unicorn's pounding gallop awakened the women from their sleep. Some women said the unicorn had the body of a deer and a twisting silver horn. Others saw the hooves of a horse or the tail of an ox. One spoke of fur sparkling with the five sacred colors—red, yellow, blue, black, and white. Another vowed that heavenly fire clothed the unicorn. I praised God for the king's good fortune. To glimpse the unicorn foretells the birth of a great being. Then, on bended knees, he pledged the fealty of a thousand generations to my glorious emperor, Chu Ti.

From the log of Cheng Ho, admiral of the western seas, voyage of the fifth armada

17

"It's a shame about the elephants," Pecheur said, bending over a piece of wood that he carefully worked on a thin vertical blade that blurred with its up-and-down speed. The saw whined and sawdust scented the air despite the powerful ventilation system.

I had been sitting in my favorite armchair in the basement workshop. I often came here to read while Pecheur drafted plans or built his models.

"Which elephants?" I asked.

"The violent ones," he replied without looking up.

"That's strange," I said. "I don't think of elephants as violent."

"Exactly."

"What's going on?" I asked.

"Herds stampede into towns, knocking down buildings, trampling anyone who gets in their way."

"Without being provoked?"

I waited for his reply. I often saw him absorbed like this, calculating, patiently working his refinements on the materials beneath his hands. Lights hooded with green glass floated above the worktable, which showed scars from long usage. On the walls hung tools such as pliers and wooden-handled screwdrivers in a dozen sizes, while the more specialized devices for building models were placed to the rear of the long table. A planking machine bent wooden strips that had been carefully soaked in water. Vises held the planking in the shape of a hull. A small wooden slip made certain the model's keel was straight and the bulkheads aligned correctly.

"They've learned to hate people," he said, straightening and turning his head to look at me. "They attack without provocation."

"Where?"

"Wherever there are wild elephants. In the last year, there have been almost a thousand of these attacks."

"There's no explanation?" I asked.

"I think they fear extinction. They're fighting back."

"But . . . "

"Futile?" Pecheur gave a grim smile. "What else can they do?"

I didn't know and didn't offer an answer. After a few moments, he picked up two masts and handed me one. "Use extra-fine sandpaper and go with the grain."

I watched as he worked the wooden surface, and I did my best to imitate his strokes. This model would be a carrack with two square sails and a triangular one to the stern. Above those sails would be topsails that caught more wind to increase the ship's speed. Large ships like these had made possible the Spanish and Portuguese voyages of exploration in the fifteenth and sixteenth centuries.

"That's enough." Pecheur reached for my dowel, examined it, and set both pieces on the worktable. "Shall we take a walk?"

At first I imagined Pecheur spent all his time in the confines of his brownstone, but in good weather, it turned out, he liked to walk in Central Park. We gathered our usual equipage in a leather backpack that I slipped over my shoulders. Soon we passed the grand buildings that overlook the park from Fifth Avenue. We entered near a playground where children run about on a thick carpet of sand. Their shouts and cries filled the air as some slid down the walls of a stone pyramid and others clambered up a tower of rope. Strolling on the paths, I glimpsed the cloudless blue sky through the branches of the wide-girthed trees. The quick breezes of April rushed about us.

Pecheur kept a steady pace. We came to flights of steps leading to a round building on a small hill. He held the railing and walked more slowly, but soon we reached the top. Stone chess tables and benches dotted the stone patio around the circumference of the building. Arbors covered with leafy vines protected the players from the sun.

Several men glanced up from their boards to greet Pecheur before returning to punching their clocks. I put the knapsack on an empty table and began to unpack—white pieces, black pieces, a chess clock, a couple of bottles of water, two greenish-gold apples. Pecheur watched the game at the next table while I set up the pieces: the queen on her own color, the castles in the corners, the knights stabled between the castles and bishops, the bishops close by the king and queen to give advice, and of course the humble pawns in front, ready to hurtle forward to doom or glory. Last I set the clock and placed it so the black player would use his right hand to make his opponent's time run. I took a bottle of water for myself and left the backpack and the fruit beside Pecheur.

"All set."

Pecheur surveyed my arrangement and nodded.

"I'll be back in a little while."

"Take your time," he answered.

I left him watching the game and walked down the steps on the far side of the small promontory. Horse-drawn carriages moved tourists slowly along the road that loops through the park. I crossed it and saw the carousel ahead. A handful of children rode up and down atop the brightly colored horses that cantered with the turning platform. Veering away, I followed the road a little distance until I came to a long, straight promenade shaded by a canopy of large trees. I walked at a leisurely pace and enjoyed the familiar statues of great explorers, authors, and composers. At the end I passed a band shell, crossed another road, and went down a long flight of steps. I sat on the stone rim of the wide fountain whose waters cascaded down over two basins from the statue of an angel with wings outspread. Ever since we'd begun our walks, with the thaws of March, I'd been coming here. The water in the large basin had a strange turbulence that I studied but couldn't explain. Looking at the angel, I felt an expectation, like a memory I couldn't quite bring to mind. Her outstretched arm seemed to point me in a direction. I felt restless and eager to move on.

After twenty minutes or so, I rose and started up a grassy embankment. This had become my unvarying route. It led me to a path that followed the border of a small lake. I headed away from the water, up a small hill, and wandered among the trees. I came to a cliff of stone and scrutinized it again. I could see cracks and small crevices but nothing more. I wanted to enter in somewhere, but I didn't know where. I had an uncanny feeling that an entrance might appear anywhere, even in the trunk of a tree. I sat on a flat stone and waited, but nothing came to mind, nothing shifted in my surroundings. At last I stood up and walked slowly back to where I had left Pecheur.

I recognized the man sitting opposite Pecheur at the stone table. Short, with curly white hair around a balding pate, he had been born in Germany near the end of the world war. The chess players came from everywhere—Russia, Israel, Tunisia, Argentina. Occasionally a Japanese man stopped by to play a few games. Pecheur would bow to him and the man would bow in return. Every day tourists flocked to the patio as if to a shrine, framing the chess players in the screens of their digital cameras.

Even though I understood only the rudiments of the game, I could see that Pecheur controlled the board and had hemmed in his opponent's king. On the clock, black digits fluttered past, marking the seconds. As soon as his opponent moved, Pecheur followed suit and built an advantage on his clock. When the game's end neared, his opponent simply studied the board as his remaining seconds vanished.

"A fine game, maestro," he said, offering his hand to Pecheur.

A conversation about the merits of the game ensued, after which Pecheur stood up. I gathered the pieces and returned them to the backpack.

"Tomorrow?" the German asked.

"Yes, tomorrow," Pecheur replied.

"For the delight of revenge . . . "

We retraced our steps but didn't leave the park where we'd entered. Instead we followed a path that descended steeply to a small lake where model sailboats glided with the winds. We sat on a bench to watch the boaters with their remote controls move the rudders and triangular sails. The breeze raised small ripples over the oval surface of the lake. Everywhere we looked the trees showed off the bright greens of their new leaves.

"It surprises me that anyone plays chess anymore," I said.

Pecheur raised his thick white brows. "Why?"

"Because computers can play chess as well as the best humans. Soon the computers will be better."

"You see it as a competition?"

"Isn't it?" I asked. "Everyone wants to win."

"That's true, yet it isn't everything."

"What do you like about it?"

"The movements of the pieces have a beauty that can only be realized in play with an opponent. There is both conflict and cooperation."

"Like in war?" I asked.

"Except that chess pieces don't suffer. As for computers, they may win games, but do they enjoy playing? I care if I win or lose, but I care more about the choreography of the pieces. If I have that satisfaction, why should I worry what a computer can do?"

He looked out to the boats gliding on the lake. After a while he shook his head as if to ward off a disturbing thought. I waited for him to speak to me, but instead he returned to the topic of chess.

"Do you know about the early chess automatons?"

"No."

"In the 1700s and 1800s several chess-playing machines were invented."

"But how could machines play chess?" I asked. "There were no computers then."

"The inventors of that time combined an interest in engineering with a curiosity about the process of thought. They built intricate machines—a mechanical ballerina might dance or a trumpeter play a march. In trying to mimic human activities, including speech, these inventors devised mechanical versions of the body. This led to breakthroughs in a number of fields. The machines were called automatons, and the chess-playing ones usually involved a human figure sitting behind a large box. The most famous was a European creation called the Turk—a figure dressed exotically to suggest that he was not part of the day-to-day world. In front of the Turk, on the top of the box, was a chessboard. The Turk's mechanical arm could lift and move his own pieces or capture and remove an opponent's."

"But it couldn't have been real."

Pecheur smiled.

"The public couldn't decide," he went on. "Before each match, a sequence of doors would be opened to reveal the inside of the box. This proved, to some at least, that a person wasn't concealed inside. One of the scientists, whose work would be a precursor to computing, said he believed the machine could think. Others reasoned that automatons could only repeat themselves, not think. They believed a child or tiny adult must be hidden inside, or that the pieces could be moved remotely by magnetism.

"But they looked inside the box."

"They argued that a person could move to different compartments as the various doors were opened. There might be false walls, to make the viewers think they had seen everything the box contained."

"If chess players had hidden inside, wouldn't one of them have given the secret away?"

"You would think so," Pecheur agreed.

"Was it real or fake?"

"You have to decide," he answered.

"But . . ."

"Of course, the automatons raised another question."

"Which is?"

"A more personal question about . . . the capacity for change. The miracle of the Turk was that he didn't simply repeat a selection of moves. People even wondered—perhaps without precisely knowing their own thoughts—if they were as adaptable as he."

"But the Turk was probably a fraud," I said.

Pecheur smiled at this.

"Anyway," I went on, "people are always changing."

"If they can think new thoughts."

"You mean the Turk was thinking?"

"What if the Turk decided he wouldn't play chess anymore—that he wanted to learn to play the piano or fall in love?"

"Wasn't he made of metal and wood?"

Pecheur waved a hand, more to ward off my comment than to agree with me. "That's undeniable," he said, and I felt I had been a bit tiresome.

He returned to watching the boats. The day had a captivating beauty built of dazzling surfaces—sunlight on ripples of water, hulls moving beneath white sails, green-leafed branches tumbling in breezes.

"Aren't they lovely?" he said after a while. "The sails are like wings."

I nodded in agreement.

"I'd like your help with something."

"What is it?" I asked.

I wanted to do whatever I could. He paid me a generous salary, more than I had earned at my marketing job. And he asked for very little. He encouraged me to read whatever I found of interest in his library. I liked to cook for him and to keep him company, but my tasks were few.

"I'm going to visit my daughter in Rome."

"Oh?"

He had mentioned his daughter from time to time, and I had seen her in some of the photographs around the apartment. Her name was Frontier, which I found strange.

"Yes, we keep in touch by phone and e-mail, but I haven't seen her in several years."

I realized that he would be leaving me in charge of the shop and building.

"Is there anything you want me to do while you're away?"

"No, nothing special. I'm not quite sure when I'll leave. In a way, much as I want to see her, I don't really want to go."

"Why?"

"I'm going to talk to her about what will happen after my death."

"But—" I started to protest.

Pecheur interrupted me. "Does that upset you?"

"Yes," I admitted.

"You're young and find death hard to discuss. She's different. After all, she's an obstetrician. And there can't be birth without death. To someone like me, whose friends are almost all gone, it's not such a difficult subject. I find myself less and less inclined to regret or grieve. Death at the end of a full life—what's tragic in that?"

"Then why don't you want to go to Rome?"

"It's not a pleasant topic, hashing over what's to happen after I'm gone. I do wonder what will happen to what I've created, what I own. The plans, the experiments, the models, and everything else. But I console myself with the fact that I enjoyed creating them. I created them for myself, I realize, as much as to better the world. For the person I was at the moment of making them but also for the person I would become later. I made myself the audience for my creations. It's easier that way."

"In that case, why worry about it? Anyway, you look healthy to me."

"That's the time to make your plans. After that . . . " He opened his hands and smiled. "It is tempting to do nothing at all, but that would be too easy. Even if the choices are hard, I want to make them as best I can. So I have an estate plan that I review and change from time to time. It includes a will, trusts, power of attorney, a health care proxy to make sure I'm not kept alive if I have no chance of recovery."

I owned nothing and rarely contemplated my own death, so I had little grasp of what shaped his decisions.

"If you're willing, I'd like you to play a role in administering the estate."

"I don't know if I'd be a good choice," I admitted. "What would it involve?"

He explained that it would be necessary to gather the property in the estate and distribute it as he had provided in the legal documents.

"Do you want to think it over?" he asked.

"No," I answered. "If you think I can do it, I'm happy to."

"You'll have professionals to help you—lawyers, accountants, whatever you need."

"Good." I felt relieved. "Frontier is your only child, right?"

"Yes."

"Won't you give everything to her?"

"She may not want a great deal of what I have."

"Does she have so much?"

"It may be important to her to have very little, even of what was mine. I want the choice to be hers."

"Why did you name her Frontier?" I had been wanting to ask him this. "I've never heard of anyone with that name."

"There must be others. When she was born, my wife and I felt it was the right name."

"How did you think of it?"

"We were on a frontier, always close to the boundary. We thought constantly about the frontier, because it seemed to be about more than geography. To us, at that time, the frontier was about possibility. If we could cross the boundary, we would make discoveries that would hold great meaning for us."

"Why couldn't you simply cross it?"

"There were forces that resisted our freedom of movement. We conceived our baby on the frontier, and she was born in the same place. So we named her Frontier."

"Where did this happen?" I asked, uncertain that I really understood.

He shrugged as if it had no importance, but I waited for his answer.

"After a while," he said, responding to an inner prompting rather than my question, "the past gathers a kind of authority. It feels futile to struggle with the way things have worked out, the decisions that were made. I have to remind myself that it wasn't always this way. That it can be changed. Even if only in how we understand what happened."

I waited for him to say more, to amplify and explain what he meant. He looked out at the sails moving on the lake.

"I did a curious thing once," he said. "A long time ago."

"What was that?"

"It was a small, maybe foolish, gesture."

"Yes?"

"When my wife died, I had to decide what to put on the marker for her grave. I was happy to say 'Beloved Wife and Mother' and add her name and the date of her birth. But I couldn't bring myself to include the date of her death. Every time I visit her grave, I think I should add when she died. But I haven't and I probably never will. When I'm gone, that's one of the things I want you to do."

18

"*H*e's ready!"

I didn't open my eyes. If I lay still in the bed, the excited voice might vanish and never disturb me again.

"He's ready!" she repeated with the same exuberance. "You have to get ready too."

Reluctantly I opened my eyes and saw her white uniform.

"Where am I?" I asked.

"The night ferry."

"This looks like a hospital room," I said. I had no recollection of making plans to travel.

"Yes, you're in the infirmary."

I touched myself through the hospital gown. My nipples felt painful and I could sense nothing below my waist. I reached down and touched my legs for reassurance. Between them my fingers found a plastic tube. I followed it until I realized it was a catheter.

"Why am I here?"

"You must be joking." She forced a quick smile. "Hurry."

"I'm not joking," I replied. "Why—"

"For a miracle!"

I didn't understand, so I tried a different question.

"What do you mean by 'hurry'? Hurry to do what?"

"To be ready."

"For what?"

"What you have to do."

"Which is?"

The nurse looked at me with reproach.

"Don't be silly. I'll go get him. Just let me do a quick check first."

She bent over me and pulled down the front of my blue gown. Quickly she squeezed the left side of my chest, then the right. Nodding with approval, she pulled the gown up to my shoulders again.

"I'm so excited for you," she said.

I wanted to protest, but she was out the door before I could speak. What did she mean by ready? I looked at my bed. Why had the safety bars been raised on each side? The top of the bed was elevated as if I might want to watch the dark screen of the television that hung from the ceiling. The curtain had been drawn three-quarters of the way around me, but I could still see a side table set to swing over my lap and a locker that might contain my clothing.

I heard the crying of a baby in the hallway. Wouldn't they have a separate maternity ward for babies? Maybe not in an infirmary. More likely a visitor had brought her baby with her. That would explain the wailing that came closer and closer to my room.

"Here he is!"

The nurse returned with a tiny, screeching bundle cradled in her arms. She came to the side of my bed to hand it to me. I glimpsed a pink, wrinkled face and tossed up my hands to ward it away.

"Take your son," she said.

"What do you mean? He's not my son. He can't be."

She looked at me with disbelief.

"Where's his mother?" I demanded, not caring about her response. "Give him to his mother."

"This child has no one but you," she said.

"You're mistaken," I answered angrily.

"I never believed what they said until this moment—you are a dreadful man." She looked ready to cry, and the squalling of the little creature had become incessant. "Unfortunately for this child, you are his only parent. His life depends on you."

"No no no, you can't intimidate me with nonsense." I wasn't going to let her burden me. "If I were the father, I would remember his mother. And I simply don't."

"Then why are you here?" Her face had turned red and she rocked the small bundle back and forth.

"I haven't any idea," I replied, "and I don't have to know. There's no need for me to prove anything."

"Isn't it odd," she asked, "to be lying in an infirmary and not know why?"

"What you're saying is impossible. That's what matters."

"There's one other little fact," she said.

"What's that?"

"This baby is hungry."

"Then feed him! He's making a racket."

"Quite."

"So?"

"The chart says he's to be breast-fed."

"Where is his mother?" I demanded with exasperation. "How many times do I have to ask you that?"

"You are his only parent," she said loudly. "How many times do I have to tell *you* that?"

"Does the hospital supply wet nurses? If it doesn't, you'll have to feed him some other way." Exhausting my limited knowledge of babies, I added, "With a bottle, I presume."

"That's not very nice. Don't listen to him," she cooed to the baby, then raised her face with an ominous expression. "I could report you to Child Services. They'll find foster parents for this ... maybe I should call him an orphan. There are people who yearn for children and can't have them. Why you should have this gift is beyond my understanding."

She scared me. What if she was right and this was my child? Would I want to be placed under a microscope by Child Services? Face endless interrogations by bureaucrats who have the power to remove the child to foster care? This baby couldn't be mine, but what if I were wrong? If I let him go, I'd have to fight with Child Services to gain custody again. By the time I realized he was mine, he might already be adopted and I would lose my parental rights forever. Wouldn't it be better to take the baby now and give him up if I learned I wasn't his father?

"May I look at him?"

The nurse pouted and twisted her torso away from me to block my view.

"Please."

This quiet word made her turn to face me and dip as if curtsying. I strained to sit farther up but couldn't. Instead I turned my head to the side and saw bright-blue eyes that stared into mine. My eyes are brown, not blue, and yet . . .

"I don't see the resemblance," I finally said.

"You have to give him time."

"There are tests," I said.

"Of course," she answered, "but he's hungry now."

"Blood types, DNA . . ."

"Nonetheless, he's crying because he's hungry."

"But what does that have to do with me?"

Holding the baby in the crook of one arm, she reached down with her free hand and lowered the top of my gown again.

"I'm going to show you how to do this," she said.

"Do what?" I asked in perplexity.

She unwrapped the baby and carefully placed him on my chest.

"He should feed eight to twelve times daily, but in two or three months the feedings will lessen. It's important to learn to do it the right way. Hold him. You have to keep his head and body straight."

I brought my hands to the warmth of his tiny torso.

"You have to touch the baby's lower lip to your nipple, like this," she continued, and began to lightly touch the middle of the baby's lower lip to my right nipple. Before I could complain, the baby's mouth gaped open. The nurse grasped me with her fingers below my nipple and her thumb above. Quickly she moved the baby so his mouth latched on to me.

"What are you doing?"

"Just relax."

"But he's . . . "

"Of course he is."

"I'm a man," I protested.

"Even expectant fathers produce hormones for milk." She spoke calmly, her voice soothing so as not to disturb either the baby or me. "Of course, you're much more than that. Unique."

"It's uncomfortable." I had no idea a baby could suck with such force.

"Give it a minute. You should get used to the sensation."

Perhaps to distract me from the voracious feeding, she continued to speak in a quiet voice.

"Make sure the baby's nose isn't blocked. If it is, raise his hips or let his head relax back slightly. Don't"—she stressed the word—"move your breast to let the baby breathe, because that can make your nipple sore. He only needs one nostril for breathing."

She had used the word "breast" and I certainly wanted to object, but I felt a gentle, pulling sensation from his lips and realized that his sucking had relieved the soreness I had felt in my . . . breast, the sense of tightness and pressure.

"If you need to take the baby off your breast, don't just lift him up. You have to put your finger between his gums to open the tight seal. If you don't, your nipples can become sore, even bruised or cracked. When one breast feels empty, move the baby to the other breast. At first the feeding won't be long, maybe three to five minutes, but later he may suck for as much as thirty minutes on each breast."

I wanted to argue, but a lassitude had come over me. I could feel the fullness of my other breast. Why hadn't I realized how uncomfortable my condition was?

"Watch."

She inserted her index finger into the corner of the baby's little mouth and separated his gums.

"Now move him to the other nipple."

I did as she told me.

"Go ahead. Rub his lip."

I did, and quickly his mouth gaped open again and I felt the initial pain as he encompassed my nipple.

"Good," she said approvingly. "Don't worry if he sucks more slowly or loses interest. Just let him feed until he's satisfied."

As I lay there, I tried to recall boarding the night ferry. I couldn't, and I had no idea what the ferry's port of origin was or destination might be. I could hear the sucking and swallowing rhythm as the baby pulled some kind of essence from me. Even if I was having trouble remembering certain facts of my existence, I knew that I was . . . and remained . . . a man, and that I could not nourish such a child. Yet he took nourishment from me. How could my knowledge, my ideas about the shapes and purposes of the sexes, overcome the tiny, warm fact of this baby at my nipple?

"The night ferry," I asked her, "where is it going?"

"It goes to a lot of places."

"But where am I going?

"I haven't seen your ticket. I really don't know."

"Where did we start from? What port?" I asked.

"There isn't a starting place. The ferry makes a circuit of cities, sometimes to the north, sometimes to south. It's in constant motion from one place to another, but the itinerary is never the same. I don't know who decides where the ship goes. I could tell you its nation of origin, but that's pretty much meaningless."

"Yes, please, what is it?"

"Liechtenstein."

As best I could recall, Liechtenstein was a tiny, landlocked tax haven.

"Can you tell me my name?"

"You're kidding me," she said, smiling pleasantly at what she imagined to be my humor. "But you do need to be thinking about names. The baby is going to need one. Do you know what you want to call him?"

I tried to think, but no names came to mind.

"I really don't know."

"We have a little book," she said brightly. "I'll find it for you."

She hurried out of the room, leaving me with the baby's warmth on my chest, his insistent pull on my nipple, and the rhythmic, gradually slowing sounds of his feeding.

"I found it," she said on her return a few minutes later. She placed a slender book on the side table and looked at the baby.

"He's finished. You have to burp him. It keeps him from spitting up and relieves bloating from swallowed air."

He had released my nipple and closed his eyes.

"Put his head here." She placed a small white towel on my shoulder. "Now you gently pat and rub his back. Like this."

She showed me by moving her hand. I began to imitate her. Soon the baby released air and a little milk.

"That's enough," she said, taking the towel and patting around his mouth. "Offer him the other nipple again, just in case he's still hungry."

I did as she said, but the baby wouldn't open his mouth.

"He's ready for a nice nap. I'm going to wrap him up and put him beside you. Keep him on his back to be safe."

"Okay." I didn't even ask why.

"Don't worry about your supply of milk. Your body will adjust to give him whatever he needs. If he's having a growth spurt, he'll want much more than usual. You'll be able to handle that. Here he is."

She wrapped him in the swaddling cloth again and placed him by my side.

"He'll probably sleep until he's ready to nurse again. I'll be back a little later."

"I can't move my legs," I said.

"Don't worry," she replied cheerily.

"They feel numb."

"Give it a little time. You'll be back to your old self soon enough."

She dimmed the ceiling lights and left us alone. A sudden fear for the baby came over me. I could feel him in the crook of my arm. So tiny. I understood why the safety bars had been raised on the sides of the bed. But what if I rolled over in my sleep and smothered or crushed him? I tried to shift from side to side but couldn't move at all. So he was safe for now.

Opening the little book, I let my eyes fall on a name at random. "Zion, Hebrew. A sign, excellent." Did that fit this baby? Honestly, who could know? I fanned the pages and alighted on another name. "Bryant, Irish. Kingly." A sign? A king? I went deeper into the book. "Kambo, African. Must work for everything." Will his life be difficult, a struggle for small rewards, fleeting joys, and even survival? I moved forward and found "Omar, Arabic/Persian. Highest, follower of the prophet, reverent." Moving toward the front, I came across "Kazuo, Japanese. Man of peace." How could I know who or what this baby might someday be? If indeed he proved to be mine, my choice of a name would only express my hopes for him.

I put the book aside, but the room held nothing to interest me. Closing my eyes, I wished for sleep or a memory, a clue. After a while, I could feel the mattress quivering. The more I focused on this vibration, the more powerful it became. I touched the bed's safety bars and felt the vibration there too. Then I realized that it must be an emanation of the engine throbbing at the heart of the ship, the engine that propelled thousands of tons of metal through the soft body of the sea.

Could he really be my son? I tightened my arm slightly about the swaddling that contained him. If he wasn't, why had they given him to me? Did it really matter? The nurse had said nothing about tests. I had mentioned them. But if I kept silent, I would have this boy as my own. He had shown his need for me, his hunger for what I could offer him. I was willing . . . I wanted to give him what I could. When this ship found a port, I decided, I would disembark with my child and start a new life.

The lights in the room brightened. I opened my eyes and saw the nurse. Had she discovered that I was not the child's father and come to take him to his mother?

"Everything okay?" She stopped by the side of the bed to look at the sleeping baby.

"Yes."

She checked the monitors. I realized that this was just a routine visit.

"Do you have children?"

"Yes." She smiled, still looking at the gauges for my vital signs. "I have a boy."

"How old?"

She turned to face me. "He's eight."

I wanted to ask her something more. "It's good, isn't it?"

"I wouldn't trade it for anything in the world," she answered firmly.

"But don't you miss him, traveling the way you do?"

"He's on the ship."

"What about school?"

"There are classes on the Internet, even for kindergarten. I teach him myself."

"And your husband? How often do you see him?"

"Every day. He's the captain."

"The captain?" At first I wondered whether to believe her, but she showed no sign of joking with me.

"Don't you miss firm ground?" I asked. "Does the ship ever stop for a month or two so you can have a change of scene?"

"Once in a while we get off the ship. But it's like a little city. We've gotten used to it. And interesting people are constantly coming and going."

"When will I be well?"

"In a few days."

"I'll be able to leave?"

"Yes."

"And the baby?"

"He could go now. He's fine."

"I don't have my passport. Does the baby need paperwork?"

"I'm sure my husband knows what to do."

"Could I speak to him?"

"He's on the bridge. I'll ask him to come when he has a break."

She lowered the lights as she left. I drifted in and out of sleep. I couldn't remember the last time I had seen daylight. Later—I must have been dreaming—I was in a palm-thatched cottage perched at the ocean's edge. I'd always wanted a parrot, and from a trader at the local market I'd bought a yellow-crested cockatoo that chattered in some foreign tongue to the boy and me.

"You asked to see me?"

I was startled by the voice and the white fluorescence of the ceiling lights. The man in the doorway looked to be about my age, wiry and certain of himself. He wore a dark uniform with golden buttons and a round white hat with a black shiny brim.

"Yes."

"How can I help you?" He came to the bedside and glanced at the tiny baby.

"We're ready to leave the ship."

"I hope you've enjoyed the voyage."

"Oh yes." I wanted to be agreeable, although I remembered nothing before waking a little while earlier. "Do you have my passport?"

"We have it in the ship's safe. You can have it whenever you're ready."

"I'm concerned about paperwork for the baby. Is there going to be red tape?"

"I don't see why there should be."

"But he has no birth certificate."

"I will prepare the documents for birth at sea. You can re-register him after that to obtain a birth certificate from the ministry."

I should have known. After all, a captain at sea has the power to join passengers in marriage, preside over births, perform final rites. But because of his power, I had feared he might raise an objection.

"Will we come to port soon?" I asked.

"In three days."

"The port, is it sunny?"

"Yes, the latitude is southerly."

"We'll disembark there," I said.

Surely I had worked before I boarded the night ferry. Wherever we landed, I would recover my skills and apply myself to earning what we would need to pay for our shelter, our food, and, eventually, my son's education. That would be the most important of all—his education. Whatever his name and whatever he might become, I wanted him to live to the fullest.

"There is one small problem," the captain said.

It had been too easy. He said the problem was small, but his words snatched the breath from my lungs.

"Yes?"

"You haven't used the full value of your ticket."

"Is there a refund?" I asked, wondering if he meant I would have difficulty being reimbursed for the unused portion of the itinerary.

"No. According to the contract you signed, there are no refunds."

"I signed a contract?"

"Yes, everyone does. You may have thought it was just a formality, but we follow the contractual provisions very closely."

"What is the problem?" I asked.

"This ship never returns to a port. Its charter forbids that."

"Why is that?"

"It's always been that way. I don't know the reason, but the implication is clear."

"Yes?" I had no inkling of what he was trying to say.

"In the contract you agreed to travel until the fare has been completely used up."

"I agreed to that?" I asked with alarm.

"Yes."

"But I want to disembark."

"And your son has no ticket."

"What are you saying?" I tried to raise myself in the bed, but I could only lift my forearms to the tops of the safety bars.

He raised his open palms to calm me.

"Please, please. These aren't insurmountable problems."

"But what's the solution?" I asked.

The captain pondered for a moment. Finally, he said, "If I allow you to disembark at our next stop, can I count on you to live up to your obligation?"

"Disembark with my son?"

"Precisely."

"What obligation?"

"That you will use up the remaining portion of your fare."

I frowned, because I didn't see how this could be done. Why couldn't I simply forfeit the balance of the fare?

"At a time of your choosing," the captain continued, "you will consult the ship's itinerary and meet us when we make landfall. The cost of your travel to that port of embarkation will not—I stress, will not—be paid for by the entity owning the night ferry. Then from that time until your ticket has been fully used up, you will remain a passenger aboard our ship."

"And my son?"

"If he wishes to journey with you, he must purchase his own ticket."

If I wanted to leave the ship, I had to agree, so I nodded my acceptance.

"Here's the document for you to sign. It amends our original agreement. Read it carefully," he said, handing me the papers.

I glanced at the lines of black type, but the words meant nothing to me.

"Does it seem to be in order?" he asked, when I rested the papers on the blanket.

"Yes."

"Excellent," he said. "We'll get this all taken care of. When you're up and about, I want you to join us for champagne in the officers' mess. A little celebration for you and the boy."

He offered me a pen. My right arm remained around the bundled baby beside me, so I took it in my left hand.

"Here," he said gently, supporting my hand with his. "If you can't write your name, the company will accept your mark."

With trembling fingers, I carefully made an X.

19

"The hospital where she works is on a tiny island called Tiberina. It's the only island in the Tiber River and it juts into the current like the prow of a ship. Two stone bridges lead to the center of Rome on one side and to Trastevere, where my daughter lives, on the other."

Pecheur and I sat facing each other in the leather armchairs. I had filled our after-dinner cups of coffee and carefully removed his old recording of *A German Requiem* from its album cover and placed it on the turntable. The grave majesty of Brahms's music filled the room. It had taken Pecheur several months to plan his trip to Rome, and then he had extended his visit and traveled to France and Holland. He looked thinner and paler than when he had left, and for his first dinner home, I had welcomed him with salmon in a sauce spiced with cumin and coriander.

"The bridges date back to the time of Caesar," he continued, "but even when those bridges were built, the island had already been a healing sanctuary for centuries. Pilgrims came to be cured by Aesculapius. They had to purify themselves before they could enter the god's sacred precincts."

"What kind of purification?" I asked.

"Bathing in the Tiber," he answered, "fasting or abstaining from certain foods, giving up wine, cleansing themselves with oil and smoke."

"Smoke?"

"In a ritual using aromatic woods and herbs. The smoke rises to the heavens." He sipped the coffee. "I felt like a pilgrim myself. There's always been a church on the site of the ancient temple. Today it's called St. Bartholomew of the Island. The altar is a magnificent porphyry bathtub that dates to Roman times. Beneath the altar are the relics of St. Bartholomew."

"His bones?" I asked.

"Yes. Well, bones believed to be his. In front of the altar is the medieval well that served as the temple's sacred spring. It's covered over now."

He paused and brought his cup to his lips. In the silence I listened more closely to the requiem. It had been recorded by the Berlin Philharmonic with a stately tempo that intensified its majesty. The swelling voices of the Choir of St. Hedwig's Cathedral surrounded us. Pecheur returned the cup to its saucer with a clink and set them on his side table.

"I spent many hours sitting in the nave of the church. At first I was impatient, eager for the workday to end so I could visit with my daughter. But after a while I began to feel calmer. I studied the murals that portrayed the highest spiritual drama. I let my thoughts drift across the span of my life. Here I was, spending my evenings with a woman I had seen born and whom I had watched grow from infant to adult. Maybe not being with her for a while made me think like this. I felt the force of life, the changes that bring us from one age to another."

"You had wanted to speak with her . . . "

"Yes, we discussed what we had to."

I waited for him to say more.

"It's curious, the way the island became a place for healing. The Romans wanted to quarantine people infected with plague. The best way was to separate them on an island like Tiberina. Only after they brought together so many sick people did they begin trying to heal them or to ease their suffering. Our hospitals grew from these ancient healing centers."

"The hospital is near the church?"

"Yes. It's called Fatebenefratelli. My daughter is in the Department of Obstetrics and Gynecology. She took me everywhere, like a tourist. To the Colosseum, the Forum, and the Pantheon; St. Peter's Basilica, the catacombs, and the Trevi Fountain. I was in Rome half a century ago. So much has changed. The crowds of visitors! The lines. She drove me out of the city to Hadrian's Villa and the ancient seaport of Ostia Antica. To have the past so much a part of the present—it gave me an odd feeling. So many lives have passed in that city. Seeing where they lived and worked, I could imagine the people who filled the streets and then passed on, as others came to take their place, to have their turn in the Eternal City."

"Here nothing is that old."

"No, of course not." He smiled and shook his head. "It was very sweet to be with my daughter."

I nodded.

"In the church," he continued, "when I had sat long enough, I could feel the water rising from that ancient spring."

"You said the well is capped."

"Yes, that's true, yet I sensed its movement up from the depths, flowing through a maze of cracks and tiny niches. In my mind, it filled the porphyry vessel with water that had been holy for thousands of years. Imagining this pooling of the sacred water soothed me in a way I can't really explain. At some point I began to recall a place I had visited many years before, a château in France."

"Which one?" I asked.

"Château de Chenonceau. It's built across the Cher River. Arches rise up from the river to support its structure. If you look from the riverbank, you can see the reflection of the château on the water. The arches blend together to make ellipses, half-real and half-mirrored. Many times I've thought I would like to sleep in a place like that, suspended above water, the current flowing beneath me. In the quiet of the church, I kept thinking of it again and again. Finally I decided to call the son of an old friend, who works in Paris for the Ministre de l'intérieur. I asked if he could arrange for me to spend one night in the château."

"What did he say?"

"At first blush—impossible. Then I explained that all my life I had wanted to do it and that I didn't know how much longer I might have to undertake such an adventure. He promised to try, though he sounded dubious. Two days later he called with the news that I would be allowed one night in the François I bedroom. I could hardly believe he had done it. The bedroom is named after the French king who slept there on two visits to the château. I scheduled my visit so I could go directly from Rome. I hadn't fully recalled the château's splendor—the extensive gardens that include a circular maze, the Renaissance furniture, the tapestries from the sixteenth and seventeenth centuries, the masterpieces by artists such as Rubens, Tintoretto, Rigaud, and van Loo. In my bedroom was a large walnut cabinet carved with a mastery that I, as a model maker, especially appreciated and admired. The cabinet's two front legs are shaped as a sea god and goddess. They have lion claws for feet, cornucopian legs and lower torsos, though their chests, arms, and heads are human. Each holds an outstretched arm to take the hand of the other.

"Alone in this ancient castle, at first I wandered through the hallways and chambers, too excited to sleep. When fatigue came over me, I settled in my bed and listened for the musical murmur of the Cher's current. I heard nothing. The château had been built too well, or too high above the river, for me to hear the water running. Disappointed, for a moment I doubted the wisdom of my visit, of my choice to make real this fantasy that in itself had always given me such pleasure. Then I slipped into sleep like a swimmer relaxing into the inky blackness of the depths. The next thing I recall is a dream so vivid that when I woke I sat up in the canopied bed."

He tipped back his cup to drink the last of the coffee.

"Would you like some more?" I asked.

He waved his hand to indicate no.

"What kind of dream?" I asked.

"I floated high above the dark side of the earth. I could see the flares of erupting volcanoes spewing lava and fiery gases like the explosions of enormous bombs. The burning inside of the earth was finding gaps to burst through to the surface of our world."

"If it was night," I asked, "could you see continents and oceans?"

"I could only see the line of volcanoes like a string of lights. The floating was pleasant, but I felt unready to be there. I can't explain why, but it was urgent that I not remain at that height. Then the dream shifted, and I found myself on a small island surrounded by the vastness of the ocean. I stood on a peak, the rest of the island falling away in dense tropical jungle. On one side I saw high cliffs with enormous waves crashing against them. On the other side a wind blew with tremendous force. I could barely stand against it. I looked for a sign of human habitation, but there was nothing. No structures, no cultivated land, no boats."

"Lonely," I said.

"I was alone," he answered, "but in the dream I didn't feel lonely. I was . . . curious."

"About what?"

"The forces, the waves and winds that buffeted this island. After I woke, the dream continued to work in me. I had the strongest impression that I could learn something from the island. Yet the dream didn't tell me what, and the island appeared to offer nothing."

I seldom remembered my dreams and, in any event, gave little thought to them. Clearly Pecheur believed in the significance of this dream.

"Slowly," he continued, "I realized where I was, in an antique bed in the François I room in the castle of Chenonceau. And I knew something else—I knew the location of the island. I had to wait a minute to make sure I wasn't still dreaming. I turned on the light they'd placed by the bedside and stood up. I recalled reading about such an island. It's in the Pacific, at the farthest boundary of the United States. Many ships have wrecked there because it's surrounded by reefs and mist. Between the heat, the constant wind, and the rainstorms that come every day, it's one of the most inhospitable places in the world."

"How did you know it was the same island?" I asked.

Pecheur studied me, his brow knit.

"The island in my dream had no latitude and longitude. If it wasn't the same island, it might as well have been. The next morning," he continued, "I spent a long time looking out the window, watching the river flow toward me and then beneath me. It made me think of my parents, myself, my daughter, her children. I had known so many rivers when I worked as a crewman after the war. I stood on decks and watched the Rhine, the Meuse, the Waal, the Nederrijn, and so many others flow beneath the ships' bows. Even the flow of my thoughts seemed to me like a river. I stayed at the window until it was time to leave Chenonceau. As if I were ending a visit with an old friend, I didn't want to leave. I took the train to Paris.

Despite pleasant memories of visits there, or perhaps because my memories were pleasant and best left unchanged, I saw nothing to gain by stopping. I made a connection straightaway for the train to Rotterdam. My parents had lived nearby, in Delft, where china is made. Rotterdam was bombed in the war and rebuilt as a modern city. Delft escaped the destruction and I found it much as I remembered it, an old town with low, quaint buildings interlaced by canals. I started in the central square, following streets that had been familiar to me as a boy.

"My walking brought me to my childhood home, a three-story house of brick with twin peaks at the top of its facade. It stood in a wall of three-, four-, and five-story buildings that face a canal lined with boats on each side. I wondered who owned it now, who lived there. I couldn't see in because lacy white curtains blocked my view. For a moment I considered knocking on the door, but I didn't really want to go inside.

"Sitting on a bench, I looked toward the harbor, where a windmill's spinning arms harvested the currents of air that blew in off the North Sea. Small motorboats moved along the canal. I could almost imagine myself in the house with my father, mother, and sister. I concentrated, to make my memories as solid as flesh, and for a few moments I felt a physical closeness to them. The family life I took for granted as a boy, never considered really, is now so far away. I even had a fantasy that I might buy the building and live there again. As if I could touch the past in that way."

"What happened to your sister?" I asked. I had seen her in the black-and-white photographs that Pecheur kept on the bureau in his bedroom.

"She died in the Hongerwinter."

"What is that?"

"The winter of famine at the end of the war."

Seeing that I still didn't understand, he continued.

"In September 1944, the Allies controlled the south of Holland. If they could capture the bridge over the Rhine at Arnhem, all of Holland would be under their control within weeks. The Dutch government in exile called a rail strike to hamper the German armies, but the Allies failed to capture the bridge. In retaliation for the rail strike, the Germans banned all food transport into the occupied areas. This included Amsterdam, Rotterdam, Haarlem, and Delft. It was terrifying to see the food disappear. By November, when the ban was lifted in part, a harsh and early winter had begun. The canals froze over, so barges couldn't bring food to us. The Germans destroyed locks and bridges to flood the countryside and stop the Allies, which made our situation worse. And the war had destroyed many of the farms. Even if there was food in the countryside, there was no way to bring it to the cities. My father and I took whatever we had—jewelry, clothing, even furniture—and walked in freezing weather to farms twenty and thirty miles away to try and trade for food. I fished through holes in the ice and trapped for what little I could catch. By February we were eating less than six hundred calories a day. The malnutrition stunted babies in the womb. If it had continued much longer, we would have all starved. At last the Germans allowed the Royal Air Force to drop food to us. By May, when we were liberated, more than thirty thousand people had died. My sister was one of them."

"I'm sorry," I said quietly. The music had finished playing. "She was younger?"

"Yes, by five years."

"It seems so unnecessary," I said.

"My small room was on the top floor, under the eaves," Pecheur said, seeming to ignore my remark. "The ceiling slanted to a peak in the room's center. My father built the wooden table where I pieced together my first model boats and airplanes from balsa wood kits. I slept in a narrow bed under a window that looked over the canal. I loved to watch the purposeful motor-boats chugging past and the sailboats gliding by like swans."

"You remember the house fondly," I said, "even though you suffered there when you were older."

"Yes, that's true." His blue eyes had a distant, reflective look that reminded me of fire and ice. "I sat on the bench for an hour or more, looking at the facade and remembering. Then I walked along the canal and through the streets until I came to the cemetery where my parents and sister are buried. There isn't much to say about my visit there, except how much I loved them. I can never thank them enough for what they gave me."

He bent his head, his eyes glistening.

"Can I do anything?"

"There's only one thing," he answered, slowly rising from his armchair.

"Yes?"

"You and I should go to the island."

"You said it's as inhospitable as any place on the planet."

"I feel there's something for us to learn there."

"But would you be able to?" I asked.

"If you go with me, I think I can."

"If you want to go," I answered, feeling how much I would prefer to go with him to Europe or anywhere that had culture, cities, history, "I'll go with you."

20

The school's corridors went on and on. Only the numbered classroom doors, with their translucent windows, broke the monotony of the gray metal lockers lining the halls. I didn't understand how corridor after corridor could be empty. Where were the students and teachers? I had to find a men's room, but there was no one to ask for directions.

At last I heard a man singing the national anthem in a tremulous voice that broke on the word "proudly." I came to an open doorway and saw a thin, pale-faced custodian of fifty or so. Dressed in a blue uniform, a bucket beside him and the handle of a mop in his hands, he sang as he cleaned. I couldn't believe my good fortune, because he was mopping the bathroom floor. I could see a row of sinks behind him, a long mirror above the sinks, and dispensers offering brown paper towels.

"Is this the men's room?" I felt I might burst.

He broke off his song and gave me a sharp look.

"What's the sign say?" he asked.

"What sign?"

He tossed his head in the direction of two interior doors. Black painted letters clearly labeled them the men's room and women's. I crossed to the men's side and pulled open the door. The shock almost made me lose control of my bladder. Two long, open rows of porcelain toilets, perhaps three dozen altogether, ran along the walls, and sitting on them in varying degrees of nudity were women, many obese, their flesh rippling in thick folds.

I backed away, closing the door behind me.

"There are women in there."

"It says it's the men's room," he responded.

"But it's filled with women."

"What do you want me to do?" he asked, leaning on the mop and studying me with his cool gray eyes.

"Tell them it's the men's room."

"You think they can't read? The sign on the door couldn't be plainer."

"I've got to go," I said in a panic. "I need a toilet, a urinal."

"You can try over there," he said with a disinterested shrug of his shoulders.

He pointed me toward the women's room.

"But that's the women's room," I protested.

"Yes?"

"I can't go in there."

"I thought you couldn't wait."

"I can't, but not in there."

"It's up to you."

I opened the door to the women's room with a prayer that it would be empty. But it looked exactly as the men's room had, filled with large women who had removed blouses, skirts, and sometimes bras. They showed no alarm at my presence and, in fact, took no notice of me. I slammed shut the door.

"Is there a private bathroom here?" I asked. "Maybe for the staff?"

He squinted as if to get me in proper focus. "You can't use it."

"Why not?"

"You're not a staff member. I know everyone on the staff. Even if you'd just come on board, you'd have a badge with your photo ID. In that case, you'd be welcome to use any of the facilities—the cafeteria, library, computer lab, and, of course, the bathrooms.

"But . . ."

It seemed to me that this should be his problem and not mine. Surely the school was required to have bathrooms available, and he, as an employee of the school, should see to it that there were.

"Can you make an exception? After all, this is a matter of human need."

"The school board has taken human need into account." He looked me straight in the eye. "It decided some people can use the staff bathrooms—that is, the staff—and some people can't. You clearly fall into the category of those who cannot."

"What if the staff bathroom is empty? Couldn't you make an exception in that case?"

"No."

"Then you should clear the women out of the men's room!" I shouted.

"That's not my job."

"Well, it should be."

"You blame anyone but yourself."

"How could I be to blame?"

"You might have planned better. You could have used a bathroom before you came here."

"What school doesn't have bathrooms?"

"We have bathrooms."

"Right," I said sarcastically, "but you don't make the women obey the rules. In effect, you have no facilities for me."

I crossed my legs, uncertain how long I could continue this back-and-forth.

"I could tell you something," he said with annoyance, "but what good would it do?"

He dipped his mop in the bucket and began weaving it back and forth on the gray cement floor.

"What is it?" I asked, shifting my weight from one foot to the other.

He looked at me.

"Why do you always give everything away?"

I shook my head.

"You're not even aware of it," he went on.

"But you are," I challenged defiantly.

"Why does the flow have to go out?" he asked.

"Because I have to pee."

"That's what you think. It's what you've always thought. Everybody has good reasons why nothing can ever change."

I wanted to tell him to get back to mopping the floor, but he didn't look like a lunatic.

"So . . . what?"

"What if the flow went in?"

"It doesn't work like that—"

"In your experience," he interpolated, to end my sentence. "What if it did? All that energy that wants to pour into the world, and that wants the world to respond and take care of you. What if it reversed itself and flowed into you?"

"Where would it go? There's only one way out of my bladder."

"Ah, the physical facts!" He raised a hand to ward off my irrelevant words. "Must everything live within the narrow confines of the physical world? Is that all we are—stomachs, guts, bladders, and the rest?"

"It's part of who we are," I insisted.

"But how does it really work? Do you know all the body's secrets, all our possibilities?"

"No, of course not."

"And your sperm," he said.

"What?"

"Your sperm. Why not take that into you as well? Why not keep its energy to feed your deepest desires and needs? The Taoist tradition encourages men to conserve their sperm."

"How is that possible?"

"By making the ejaculation flow inward."

"But to where?" I asked.

"'Where' in this case isn't a physical place," he answered. "It's a metaphor."

"But it has to go somewhere. If it doesn't go out, where does it go inside the body?"

"Literally," he paused, "it goes backward, into the bladder. But the Taoists believe that unspent semen travels up the spine and nourishes the brain. It builds the good energy that brings health, perhaps even immortality."

"What kind of custodian are you?" I demanded.

"Are the hallways clean?"

"Yes." I had to admit that.

"Are the bathrooms well maintained? Are there paper towels in the dispensers?" He gestured about the room. "And soap and toilet paper?"

"Yes."

"There's your answer."

"But . . ."

He began mopping again.

"What are you talking about?" I finally got out. "It makes no sense. No one is immortal. And no one will become immortal or even healthy by holding back their sperm."

"You have proof?"

He looked concerned, and I realized that I might have brought into question one of his deeply held beliefs. Regret overcame me. What right did I have to shake his certainties?

"No, I have no proof, none at all."

"I didn't think so," he said with an injured look. He returned to mopping patterns on the floor.

I heard screams from the men's room. The custodian continued to mop as if he heard nothing, but I rushed to the door. A teenage boy had appeared from I don't know where and was kneeling over a slender, red-haired girl who trembled on the floor in some kind of fit. Ignoring the half-naked women, I rushed forward.

"Shall we call for help?" I asked the young man.

He held her shuddering shoulders and studied her face. I saw that he was handsome and well built, his skin smooth and his cheeks pink with the flush of youthful health.

"No," he said, gently releasing her as the tremors lessened, "she'll be all right."

"You're sure?" I asked.

"Yes."

He didn't seem concerned, and I decided that he must know best. The girl, her skin ever so white on the red pillow of her hair, slipped into a peaceful sleep. The woman nearest me was holding up a small mirror and carefully using tweezers to pluck at hairs I couldn't see. I turned away and exited the room. I didn't stop when I came to the custodian but hurried forward into the main corridor.

"Where are you going?"

The young man followed me.

"I'm looking for a bathroom," I said urgently.

"Didn't you come here to speak?" he asked.

Could he be right? Had I? If so, what topic had I selected? I kept silent and walked at a furious pace back along the corridor. The youth skipped every dozen or so paces to keep up with me.

"I want to hear what you're going to say," he continued. "How do you know what to do? How does anyone make a choice?"

"You have nothing but possibilities," I said, envying him the freedom of youth when nothing is yet shaped or definite.

"That's not enough."

He touched me because possibility has such beauty, and yet what he said was true. He couldn't remain forever in the possible. He had to choose one way or another. He would make choices, and each choice would move him more definitely along a path that would be difficult to erase.

"How did you choose your career?" he asked.

"By accident," I replied.

"What?" He looked dubious.

I started to walk again but more slowly. The boy kept pace with me as we passed the gray lockers and turned into another corridor, identical to the last.

"I did something for a long time," I said, not recollecting exactly what but feeling that I spoke the truth, "and that became my career."

"Didn't you need training?" he demanded. "Maybe a degree? Or were you an apprentice? Doing something for a long time sounds like . . . like you didn't think about it before you started. But you have to know where you want to go. If you don't think before you start, how can you ever get there?"

What he said, and the innocence and intensity with which he said it, made me believe him. If I had intended to say anything different, I would have been a very poor speaker. It would be just as well if I didn't speak.

"If you do something long enough," I answered despite my thoughts, "you essentially give up all the other possibilities."

"That doesn't sound like career guidance."

"Maybe it's not," I admitted.

He stopped at a door indistinguishable from all the rest.

"Don't let them hear you talk like that."

"Who?" I asked.

"The committee. It has to finish its review before you can give your talk."

With that, he opened the door to a classroom where a dozen men and women sat at a long table. Abruptly I recalled having been there only a few minutes before, ready to speak, when the need to use the bathroom had overcome me. One of the women, the chairperson, nodded to welcome me back and gestured with her hand that I should take a place at the head of the table.

"Please continue," she said.

I leapt somewhere into the middle of the talk I imagined I'd begun.

"It's not to seek the goal that we can imagine," I said passionately, "but to seek what is unimaginable. We can describe innumerable paths to careers, but can we find the secret paths to happiness? If you were to take the most successful among us, wouldn't they remember a time when anything was still possible? The scientist might have been a teacher. The teacher might have been a doctor. So many opportunities are foreclosed by the very choices that let us climb the ladder of success. Is there a secret antidote for this loss?"

I looked at their faces. They gave no sign of response. Was I speaking only to myself? Yet with or without their encouragement, the stream of words poured out of me.

"Remember the dreams of your youth," I said, my earnestness causing me to skip much that I might have said. "Remember youthful pleasures. Never give up your imagination. Why should moving forward be giving up? It doesn't have to be! Whatever your career, hold tightly to the joys of your youth."

I continued until my flow of words trickled to silence. I glanced from face to face, but they all looked down at their writing pads or fiddled with their pens.

"I like to choose my words carefully," the chairwoman said after a pause, "and, in this case, brevity has a great deal to commend it. So, in place of my usual detailed critique, I'll offer one or two carefully chosen words."

I noticed that her cheeks had flushed. I could feel my voice still vibrating in the room.

"Preposterous," she said sharply, "and ridiculous!"

Sadness for her came over me. Her professional status squeezed her ever so tightly into herself. It would be futile to remind her of the possibilities that had once been hers or to plead with her to recollect her early dreams and pleasures. The others nodded in approval.

"He shows no grasp of what our students need to hear," said a portly, balding man who looked over his eyeglasses to his colleagues.

"In fact," added a tall, intense woman with jabs of her index finger, "his message is the diametric opposite of what we believe.

Career success is the result of application and hard work, not fantasy and escapism."

"All things considered," observed a heavyset man with salt-and-pepper hair, "he would be best served by listening to exactly the type of lecture he was supposed to give here."

They went on speaking about me to each other, but no one addressed me in person. They acted as if I had left the room or become the subject of a study. Their conversation absorbed them, and no one objected when I crept out of the room.

"Did you hear any of that?" I asked the youth in the hallway.

"No."

"I won't be invited to speak—that's for sure."

We began to walk down the corridor, but I lost all sense of direction. The meeting lingered with me, and I wasn't sure whether we were returning the way I came or going a different way.

"Here's a bathroom."

"Staff" was painted in dark letters, at eye level, on the wooden door.

"I can't use that."

"Why not?"

I waved at the letters.

"Go ahead," he said. "I'll stand guard."

"What if we get caught?" I asked.

"Maybe they'll expel me again," he answered cheerfully.

"Again?"

"Yes, I was missing for quite a while."

"Missing?"

"I ran away. First they expelled me for poor attendance. Then when months went by and I didn't show up, people got really upset . . . "

"Especially your parents."

"Sure. My picture ended up everywhere—on posters, milk cartons, TV shows, you name it."

"Did they find you?"

"Nope."

I hesitated.

"Okay," I said.

He smiled and ushered me forward with a wave of his hand. I entered the bathroom, locked the door behind me, positioned myself in front of the toilet, and began to urinate. Well past the moment when the flow would normally have stopped, it simply continued like a flood. I filled the toilet to its brim and had to reach forward and flush it to prevent a spillover, and still the urine poured out of me until I flushed again, and continued until I flushed once more and was finally empty. I kept thinking about the youth waiting outside. I wanted to ask him questions, but I wasn't sure where to start. Feeling much better, I zipped my trousers and stepped into the hallway.

"All set?" he asked

"Yes, thanks."

"Come on."

He pointed down the corridor, and we started walking again.

"Where did you travel?" I asked.

"Mexico to start. Then I went south—Guatemala, Honduras, Nicaragua, Costa Rica."

"Was there a reason?"

"To run away?"

"Yes."

"For fun."

"But people worried. Your parents must have worried."

He shrugged.

"Was it?" I asked.

"Yeah, sure. I mean, of course it wasn't all fun."

"No?"

"When I got bored, I came home. So here I am."

"Why Mexico?" I asked.

"I could get there. No way could I get to Europe or some-place like that."

We reached a main entrance with three revolving doors.

"Here you are," he said.

"Do you play ball?" I asked, not wanting to let him go.

"Sure," he smiled.

"Baseball?"

He nodded.

"Let me guess. You're the third baseman."

"Close, shortstop."

He seemed perfectly willing to stay and chat with me, but I worried that he might be missing a class.

"So long," I said after a few more questions and answers.

"Adios," he answered, and turned to walk down the corridor.

I wanted to call him back. Was there something more to say or do with him? He never looked back. Rounding a corner, he left my sight. I lingered in the hallway, although I had no reason to believe he would return. I didn't know how long I would wait. Why hadn't I called to him? I felt so . . . incomplete.

21

I had been living with Pecheur for nearly two years when his health began to decline. Not long after visiting with his daughter in Rome, he complained of pain in his hands and feet. I didn't feel it a burden to take him to doctors' appointments and keep track of his medications. He hadn't lost his acuity and could have managed the pills by himself, but I wanted to help in whatever way I could. I took him to the hospital for a series of tests, but the inconclusive results were followed by several more stays during which the causes of other discomforts remained equally mysterious. He suffered from dizziness that came and went, and would remain in bed on those days with books piled up around him.

By this time I had learned a great deal about his life and interests. If he needed to spend the day in bed, I would bring him his breakfast on a tray. I would comb through his collection of old records and play his favorites, such as Britten's opera *Billy Budd* and Mahler's Ninth Symphony.

Despite the difficulties with his health, Pecheur set to work soon after his return from Europe. In the third-floor gallery, I helped him take down the panorama of the coastline that resembled Holland. We stored the physical pieces in a large room off the basement workshop, where I could see the covered shapes of other projects that had been completed and put away before I became his assistant. To me the magic had been in the computer programming that made the seas surge and fall back, and I wondered what animated the models that he made without computers and advanced electronics. In any event, we soon cleared the gallery and began the construction of the island of his dream.

"It's a stratovolcano," he told me, "with magma of high viscosity. Its explosive force is immense. The volcano itself is tall and steep, because the lava is brittle and molten rock is forced up and hardens on the slopes. Judging from the angle of incline, this island was formed by multiple eruptions that finally drove the tip of the volcano above the waves."

"Could it erupt again?" I asked.

"It certainly could." He pointed to the peak of the volcano. "Here is the magma cap. It's created by the slow extrusion of magma from the core. These volcanoes occur in chains as tectonic plates collide and slide over one another. The Ring of

Fire comprises a thousand volcanoes that rim the Pacific Ocean. The volcano on our island is unusual because it's solitary."

Pecheur selected and scaled his materials with a care that bordered on obsession. He had sources that supplied him with pumice from the eruption of Mount Pinatubo in the Philippines. From elsewhere he gathered the two common types of lava, one smooth and flat like a roadway surface and the other made of jagged individual rocks. He ordered some lava flecked with olivine, a semiprecious stone. He also located sand made from the wearing away of this lava. The sand, which he used for the island's beaches, had a greenish tint. I wondered whether his dream had such specificity, or whether he simply used his imagination to create the barren, volcanic outcrop that rose in the gallery. He took pains to build a vent within the volcano where the magma would rise, and he worked the stony slopes to create the strata layered by eruptions over millions of years. He surrounded the island with jagged reefs like a serrated crown.

"It's coral," he replied when I asked what he used to make the gleaming pink and black of the reefs. "Coral reefs form around these volcanic islands. The islands rise up because of the magma and ash, but later they settle as the oceanic crust adjusts to the weight. If the islands sink enough, the reefs enclose lagoons."

At this critical juncture, with the physical setting complete but the programming hardly begun, Pecheur stopped work because of his worsening health. He suffered shortness of breath, vertigo, and weakness. At some moments he felt that he would lose all control over his body. At his instruction, I employed nurses around the clock. Occasionally he would walk with a cane to survey the island, but on most days the nurse on duty would roll him around in a wheelchair to gaze at the work that had halted.

"This is an impossible island," Pecheur said to me. "We have to program for fierce currents, towering waves, and an enormous undertow."

It cheered me to hear him speak of continuing the project, but within another few weeks, he stopped speaking of what he planned and hoped to do. He looked shrunken in the wheelchair, fatigued and sallow.

"I can't keep my mind off this," he said, gesturing toward the large basin. It held a roundish island about five feet in diameter that rose to a mountain peak with flanks covered by rain forest. Palm trees stood in thick clusters near the skirt of beaches, but there was no ocean, and nothing in the tableau moved.

I stood quietly beside him. I didn't have to speak because both he and I knew what he said was true. He didn't rest easily in his sickbed and always wanted to come here.

"I've been having a lot of thoughts," he said.

"Yes?" I wondered if he had someone in mind who might help us finish his work or, less likely, if he had decided to admit that it would remain incomplete.

"I'd like you to go to the island."

"Without you?"

"Yes." He smiled wanly. "I'd like you to go and report back to me. Tell me what you find there."

I didn't want to go. I didn't know what he hoped to discover there; I would simply be visiting a place of desolation. But I also respected whatever drew him to the island. He had so often let himself be guided in this way.

"Shouldn't I stay here and help?" I asked.

He shook his head.

"Go and tell me what you discover."

I made plane reservations and chartered a boat with an experienced captain, but Pecheur returned to the hospital. Day after day, as I debated whether to stay with him or go as he wished, he weakened. Soon he lacked the strength to move or speak. In the end, the decision was taken away from me. Pecheur died. I postponed the trip. And even my grief at times was pushed aside by the funeral arrangements and innumerable other practicalities that became my responsibility.

I made certain that he was buried as he wished, beside his wife, on a promontory overlooking the Atlantic. To his wife's headstone I added the date of her death. His headstone merely has the name he chose, Pecheur, and the dates of his birth and death. Behind the graves stands a grove of pine trees, old and tall and green in every season. The surf breaks on the beach below, and the breezes carry the scent of the pines and the ocean.

Pecheur made me his heir and his trustee. I owned the Floating World, the building that housed it, and many other properties and assets. The model boats remained on their pedestals in the glow of the spotlights. I liked to walk among them and study the intricacy of their details and the fineness of their workmanship. At one point, curious about Pecheur's name for the shop, I discovered that the floating world was about far more than illicit pleasure. Called *ukiyo* in Japanese, it grew out of the Buddhist concept of a world filled with pain and came to mean the transient and unreliable nature of our world, how fleetingly it floats in the illusion of time. I decided to turn the building into a museum and open it to the public.

Pecheur had been involved in supporting many causes, and I continued his good work. As the trustee of his foundation, I donated money to feed the hungry, to support dance companies and orchestras, to remove mines from old battlefields, to make small loans to impoverished people who dreamed of being entrepreneurs, to fund scholarships, to fight diseases, to preserve the environment, to aid the elderly, and much more. I tried as best I could to support scientific research that would advance Pecheur's dream of harmonizing the forces of nature.

Often I returned to the third-floor gallery and studied the model of the island with its volcano. I hired programmers to make waves beat against the reefs and a dark cloud of smoke billow above the peak, but the essential mystery Pecheur sought eluded me. Sitting at the controls, I wanted to take the next step. I kept recalling his request that I visit the island. If he had lived, I would certainly have gone, but even now, after his death, it felt like something unfinished. I didn't want to go for myself but I wanted to do it for Pecheur. Finally, hoping that the trip might be more pleasant than I imagined, I chartered the boat for a two-week voyage, rebooked my plane tickets, and readied myself to leave.

The four black bears came at night. I woke to the sound of huffing and grunting and a familiar pungent scent, like hay drying in a barn but much stronger. Propping myself up on my elbows, I managed to open my eyes and saw the bears prowling around my room.

"What's going on?" I demanded.

"Do you always sleep with the lights on?" asked one of the smaller bears.

"Scared of the dark?" jeered another who, as far as I could tell, looked exactly like the first.

"Who let you in?"

"You left a key for us," said the first. "Don't you remember?"

"That's ridiculous." I sat upright. "I didn't leave keys for anybody."

"Then how did we get in?" he asked.

No answer came to mind, which didn't mean he was right. I had been in a deep sleep and hadn't really awakened yet.

One of them sniffed at my foot, then licked it, and I jerked away.

"Cut it out."

"Did he say, 'Cut it off'?" asked the second bear in his jeering tone.

"Mind your manners," said one of the larger bears. I could tell from the timbre of the voice and the gentleness of the admonition that she was the mother of the two smaller bears.

The biggest bear—he must have weighed six hundred pounds—stood up on his hind legs. Obviously this was the father, so my visitors were not a sleuth of random bears but a family.

"It's a matter of mutual obligation," the huge bear said in a deep, gravelly voice.

"Whose mutual obligation?" I asked.

"Yours and ours."

"What obligations can we possibly have? I don't even know you."

The mother bear put a large paw on my leg to hold me in place.

"What are you doing?" I asked her.

"We have to eat you," the father bear replied.

"Eat me?"

"Yes."

I squirmed as more paws pressed me down on the mattress. A tongue wetly touched my foot, and I felt the gnawing of sharply pointed teeth.

"Why?" I asked, suddenly awake in a way I had never been before. I couldn't believe what he was saying, yet there they were in my bedroom. And one of them had my foot in his mouth.

"We're famished." His dark eyes had a mournful look.

"You don't look famished," I answered. "Judging by your size, it looks as if you've been eating plenty."

"We really have no choice."

"You do have a choice," I pleaded. "Look in my refrigerator. Eat what's there."

"We already looked," said one of the smaller bears. "Who can live on a few bottles of beer and a jar of pickles?"

I felt teeth closing like a vise on my foot. I tried to shake free, but I couldn't move. My heart leapt in my chest. Then a terrible pain shot up my leg. I raised my head just enough to see blood pouring from my ankle and the two small bears chewing on my severed foot.

"Stop!" I screamed. "It's not too late. You can leave and I'll go to a hospital. I'll say I had an accident. I won't tell anybody."

"Shut up," one of the small bears said in a disrespectful tone.

"That was bony," complained the other small bear as he yanked at the flesh of my right arm. I could feel the furrows left by his teeth and the wetness of my blood pouring forth. Other jaws ripped a chunk from my left thigh and more blood pooled underneath me.

"I don't want to die," I whimpered.

"Don't think of it as dying," the father bear said with an encouraging tone. "Think of it as becoming one of us. Your flesh will nurture us. You'll become part of us."

"I don't want to be a bear."

"And we will become more human."

"But you're bears!" I screamed in confusion and pain.

"Better to say that we're not fully bears," he replied. "And you're not fully human."

"But you'll be alive and I won't."

"Don't be so literal," one of the smaller bears said as he licked rivulets of blood from his dark lips.

"At least let me be cooked," I pleaded, hoping for any delay.

"You think you're the only one making a sacrifice?" asked the smaller bear. "You think we like eating people, cooked or otherwise? My mealtime favorites are berries, herbs and grasses, insects, and maybe an occasional rat or rabbit."

To be devoured piece by piece flooded me with terror. It would be better to be already dead, not living in the expectation of further torment.

I was about to reply when powerful jaws clamped on my femur and ripped my leg away from the trunk of my body. A spray of bright-red droplets covered the white walls and ceiling.

"Forgive us," said the largest bear.

A tongue licked my cheek, teeth touched against my fleshy stomach. Soon I would have no face, and my entrails would be spread across the carpeting. I must have gone into shock at last, because the pain began to lessen.

Then I was floating near the ceiling of my room. Beneath me the bears were gnawing on my remains. I was peaceful there and untroubled by such fleeting thoughts as there could have been more to my life, I might have achieved more, or I might have been a better husband. If I could have done things like that, maybe I would have opened the fridge, poured tall glasses of golden beer, passed them from paw to paw, wrestled the bears to exhaustion, demanded back my keys, or even asked for their forgiveness for reasons I couldn't quite bring to mind. In any event, I was no longer worried about the body that once contained me. Just thankful that it had served me well, and for the extra roll of flesh around my middle that would help relieve their terrible hunger. I didn't understand the bears, but the beauty of it was that I no longer had to.

*H*armony, *good fortune, and, above all, fertility are the unicorn's gifts. Easily able to outrun its pursuer and avoid net, trap, or arrow, the unicorn will come tamely from the deepest forests to rest its horned head on a virgin's lap. Though neither man nor woman, I am a virgin of sorts. In my heart most of all. If the unicorn judges me unworthy, let his horn enter my navel and rip its way to that heart. Or let it rest its head in my lap and make me as I once was. Removing my garments, I reveal my scar. All day I wait, watching but seeing nothing. At twilight the rustling begins, close to me on one side and then the other, circling, coming closer until the darkness brings the moon and stars quivering above me.*

From the log of Cheng Ho, admiral of the western seas, voyage of the fifth armada

*T*he small, hunched man peed in the waves rushing over his feet. In the wash of the silver moonlight, I could see that he was naked. The first long spurt subsided and his flow trickled to a halt. He tugged a few times on his penis and let his hands drop to his sides, then remained like a patient sentry looking out over the moonlit ocean.

"Where . . ."

I couldn't say more, at first, through my parched throat. My head throbbed.

"Where am I?"

I spoke louder on my second try.

The man turned to face me. Now I could see that he was Japanese and very old, perhaps eighty or ninety, with a sparse goatee and long, unkempt white hair fringing his bald pate. He couldn't have weighed even a hundred pounds. Wrinkles puckered his face and the skin below his navel draped in loose folds.

"You don't know where you are?"

I could barely understand the strange, slow drawl in which he spoke English.

"No," I gasped.

"Clever, very clever."

"Why?" My voice came in a whisper.

"Where is your uniform?"

I shook my head.

"What is your unit?" he asked.

Again I didn't understand him and shook my head.

"You were separated from the rest of them?"

"Yes," I replied, recollecting a ship and a crew.

He walked a few steps closer to me and looked me up and down, his dark eyes at once stern and suspicious.

"Liar." He nearly spit the word.

"What?"

"You are," he paused, "a deserter."

"From what?" I managed to ask.

"You don't know?" He looked crafty, disbelieving.

"No."

"There were others with you," he asserted.

"Yes, the crew."

"They sent you here."

"No."

"Give me their position and numbers."

"I can't."

"Tell me!" He stepped forward and raised his voice.

I tried to lift myself up from the sand but felt too weak. My body ached everywhere.

"Water," I said, "please."

The man kicked the moving water so it splashed in my face.

"Where are they?" he demanded.

"Water. I can't speak."

Shaking his head, the man reached to pick up a plastic bottle without a top and handed it roughly to me. I tipped it up so the little water gathered in its bottom wet my lips, tongue, and throat.

"Where are the others?" he said again.

"Dead," I spoke louder now, "drowned. Or maybe they were rescued. I don't know."

"Are they on the island?"

"I don't know. What day is it? "

He stood above me, studying me, not answering.

"How long have I been here?" I asked.

"I pulled you from the water three days ago," he said. "I protected you from the sun with that."

He pointed behind me. Turning painfully, I saw a small lean-to.

"Now you answer my questions," he continued. "Navy?"

"What do you mean?" I couldn't believe I had been unconscious for three days and this strange man had saved my life.

"Was it a navy boat?"

"No." I began to remember more. "I chartered the boat. A storm came up, a typhoon with a spout of spinning water that would have knocked down a skyscraper. It broke the boat apart.

I don't know what happened to the others. I guess I was washed ashore here."

"Chartered?"

He could hardly pronounce the word. I suspected he had no idea what it meant.

"I rented the boat. It didn't belong to me."

"I could have killed you many times."

I almost laughed. This minuscule man . . . why would he even think of killing me? Yet his eyes expressed a certainty that worried me.

"What are you saying?"

"You look like the enemy."

"What?"

He gestured toward my face and body. I realized that I wore nothing and was as naked as my rescuer. The waves crashed and receded a few feet from us.

"You speak his language. Even if you have no unit and no uniform, you may be a spy."

"I'm the survivor of a shipwreck!"

"So you say."

"Thank you for rescuing me."

He considered this for a little while and then spoke more calmly.

"I will treat you as a noncombatant for now."

"Where is the war?" I asked. Slowly I managed to sit upright.

"Everywhere." He gestured toward the bright constellations above us.

Could a war have begun in the last few days?

"Who is at war?"

"You don't know?"

"No."

"What is your country?"

"The United States."

"You are at war with Japan."

I looked at him for a smile, a hint that he joked with me.

"How long have you been here?" I asked.

"Since 1944."

"Haven't any boats landed here in all those years?" I asked.

"If I saw boats or planes, I hid in the rocks. There are caves."

"The war ended in 1945."

"You are mistaken."

"In August 1945 the emperor surrendered. Japan became a peaceful country, a democracy."

He smiled at the impossibility of what I said.

"You have no radio?" I asked.

"The emperor would never surrender."

"Terrible bombs were dropped on Hiroshima and Nagasaki. The cities were destroyed, and more than a hundred thousand people lost their lives. Then the emperor surrendered."

"No bomb can destroy a city."

"Even Tokyo was destroyed by fleets of bombers that came again and again. It was leveled."

He smiled a superior smile, his face silvery in the bright light of the moon. Obviously he judged me to be a lunatic or a liar.

"Why don't you see battleships or bombers anymore?" I probed.

"Here we are victorious. The war has shifted to other sectors. Perhaps you Americans are fighting us in California or Arizona."

How could I convince him? If I had a radio, a television set, or access to the Internet, I could have shown him a new world beyond his imagining. Or if I could go to a library, innumerable books would prove what I said. But neither the surf nor the moonlight contradicted him or supported my version of the facts.

"Even if you are a soldier or a spy," he went on, "you may be able to help us."

"There's someone else?"

"Yes, my prisoner."

"Prisoner? Who is he?"

"A member of your armed forces."

"How long has he been a prisoner?"

"Since 1945," he answered in a matter-of-fact way, "but you will be my guest."

"What kind of help do you want?"

"You will see."

If he had been alone, I might not have gone with him. It was the promise of meeting this other, the prisoner, that made me stand and walk unsteadily behind him as the surf rushed in foaming crescents over the moonlit beach.

he light on my miner's hat shone like a third eye that let me see in the darkness of the caves and fissures within the volcano. I walked downward, sometimes hunching over and other times crawling on my hands and knees. At last the rocks tightened around me and I had to shed my backpack and clothes to slither forward on my gut. Now I wore only my miner's hat, underwear, socks, and boots.

"Have you come to visit me?" A woman's voice reverberated off the stony walls.

I moved my head back and forth, but the beam of light only penetrated twenty or thirty feet, and I couldn't see her.

"Where are you?" I called out.

"Here!" Her voice echoed from every direction.

"Let me see you."

She laughed, a tinkling vibration that grew until I feared the walls around me might shatter.

"What have you lost?"

"Why?" I asked. "Why do you say that?"

"What have you come for?" she asked again. "The diamonds in the blue veins? Or perhaps to see someone? To take someone with you, back the long way you have come?" Again the laughter rose uncontrollably.

"Who are you?" I asked.

A woman—I'll call her that—stepped forward into the beam of my light. She wore nothing, and her flesh was not flesh. She might have been shaped from an enormous ruby, and she shone with a red glow unlike any I had seen. She started to move her hips, and her arms undulated as her bright eyes fixed on me. Slowly, deliberately, she danced in the illumination of her own fantastic light. She could not be a woman and yet she had a woman's shape. Her breasts were ample, her waist tapered above the fullness of her thighs and buttocks. Her little feet pressed ever so precisely to the stony floor. I had seen belly dancers move their bodies with such art and vigor that a divine vibration seemed to enter them. But this woman *was* that vibration. She moved because the vibration moved. She danced the dance of the vibration. And I imagined I heard—it could not have been real—an indescribable music, beautiful and penetrating. Somehow I knew that she did not dance to the music; her movements created the music. For all its beauty, it lived only for the moments of her moving.

She stopped, her bright eyes glowing and piercing into every recess within me. She knew what I knew, even what I had forgotten. I couldn't think, much less speak.

"My name is Numun," she said in a quiet voice.

"Why?" I barely croaked the syllable, and had no idea what question I wanted to ask her. Why did she have a body at once like a woman and a radiant gem? Why did she confront me? Why was she here, at this great depth?

"Why are you here?" Her inflection made it clear that she asked this for me and not for herself. "Weren't you warned not to come?"

I shook my head. I had no recollection of a warning.

She raised her right hand with her palm cupped and her fingers spread. I could tell this had a meaning, but I had no idea what it was.

"Go back."

I wanted to do as she told me. The light cycled upward in her body and emerged from the top of her skull like a radiant crown. I had no reason not to do what she ordered. Yet I stood there, unable to go back.

"I can't," I finally answered.

She smiled, but I didn't find her expression pleasant.

"Whom have you come for?" she asked.

"I don't know."

"Think."

I tried, but her shimmering closeness unnerved me.

"You have a memory of someone."

I struggled to focus, but no image came to mind.

I could feel the certainty that had brought me this far, the certainty that I had still farther to go. I tried to remember the reason, but the effort dizzied me.

"Go back," she said again.

She waited for my response.

"What is green in your world," she went on when I didn't speak, "is golden here. Nothing will be as you imagine it or as you want it to be. Go back."

I gave a small shake of my head.

Her face tilted to the side as if to see me from a different perspective.

"Then take this."

She flipped a small coin that tumbled end over end until I caught it . . .

26

"Hey, kid, did you get a good night's sleep?"

I opened my eyes to see the prisoner squatting next to me. Hearing his accent, I knew where his captor had learned English. What he actually and very slowly said sounded much more like, "Hey, kee-uhd, did yew git a good naht's sleep?"

I sat up, looking around me. I ached but at least I could move.

"I hear you're from America," he said, pronouncing it "Amur-cah."

"Yes."

"Bet you're hungry. We got you some food here and water." He pointed to another plastic bottle and a few morsels of food on a flat stone.

I drank first, then bent forward to eat.

"What is this?" I finally asked.

"Clams, slugs, a couple of big insects, a little bit of fish, and a little bit of snake. We preserve everything in brine."

That explained the salty taste, but I ate without caring.

"Where are you from?" he asked. "What state?"

The prisoner was a large man with wide hips and white hair that cascaded from his head and face and curled from his chest to his genitals. His ears looked like saucers as they poked out from the white hair that fell to his shoulders. His brown eyes shone warmly over the long bridge of his nose. Gentleness showed in his speech and even the way he came near without crowding me.

"New York."

He smiled with pleasure.

"I never met anyone from New York before. That's what I'm going to call you, New York. And you call me Tex."

He offered me his large hand. My smaller one clasped it for a shake.

"This is your camp?" I asked.

Large boulders formed a basin around the patch of sand where I had slept.

"Yep, the cave is dry. That's good. From here there's nothing but fields of stone going all the way to the top. Some days I've seen enough smoke to wonder if it's going to blow again right then and there."

I looked and saw a spiral of smoke rising from the volcano's crater.

"You have fire?"

He shook his head. "Tsukino-san is afraid of fire. He doesn't want to give our position away."

"Tsukino-san?"

"Yes, that's his name."

"He claims the war has moved away from here. So why is he afraid?"

Tex shrugged.

"Damned if I know."

"Where is he?" I asked.

"He's goes out and pokes around."

"You know the war is over," I said.

"No, I didn't know that," he said with a frown. "Who won?"

"We did," I answered. "And it ended a long time ago, in 1945."

"You don't say." He shook his head in amazement.

"So you're not a prisoner anymore."

"He told you that, did he?"

"Yes."

Tex considered this.

"Really we're both prisoners of this island. That's the truth. It looks like you are too."

I nodded.

"You know, New York, happy as I am to see you, I feel sorry for you too. The boys and I used to talk about islands that were like paradise. Beautiful women, fruit hanging ready to eat from the branches, no mess halls or rations from a can. What if I had ended up on one of those islands? But you, me, and Tsukino-san pulled the short straws. That's how it goes."

"How'd you get here?"

"Plane crash."

"What kind of plane?"

"I was tail gunner in a B-24. They called them flying coffins. Those planes only had one exit—out the rear. The catwalk to get there was so narrow you could hardly move with your parachute on. The fuel tanks like as not would go up in flames if the plane got hit. One day it happened. We were out in formation. Zeros came overhead. Machine gun rounds ripped through our right wing. Sure enough, the fuel tanks caught fire. We tried to fight it, but finally the captain said jump. I was the first one out. As I came down, I could see black smoke pouring off the wing. The plane kept going closer and closer to the ocean. I didn't see anyone else parachute, but I didn't see it crash either. To this day, I keep hoping those boys are okay."

"How did you and Tsukino-san meet up?"

"The winds blew me into the rocks. Split my head open and knocked me out. When I woke up, I couldn't move. The parachute was tangled. The waves were like a thousand hands trying to pull me out to sea. I didn't know it, but the tide was rising. By all rights I was a dead man. Then Tsukino-san shows up. He opened my harness and dragged me out of the water. In those days he was one strong fellow. Once he got me far enough up the beach, he went back for my parachute."

"He rescued me too," I said.

"Then he started spouting off in Japanese. I didn't know what he was talking about. Took a long time for him to learn

English and for me to learn some Japanese. We practiced at it, like we were at some school for languages. Didn't have a lot else to do. He taught me to play go. We spent a lot of time doing that. Anyway, eventually we could communicate well enough for me to understand that I was his prisoner. He waved his knife around and scared the hell out of me to prove the point. I'd heard a lot about what the Japanese did to Americans. Cutting limbs off prisoners to eat, while keeping them alive so they'd still have fresh meat."

What I knew came from history books. I had read of atrocities but nothing like this.

"I don't believe that," I said. "It's too inhuman. You're just repeating rumors."

"You can call them rumors if you want to. But when Tsukino-san raised his knife, I believed everything I ever heard."

"You're still here, so he didn't use the knife."

"Actually, he took great care of me. Cleaned and dressed my head wound, fed me as best he could."

At that moment Tsukino-san appeared on the rim of the rock basin. He slipped down through the crevices between the boulders with the ease of a younger man.

"Are you ready to go?" he asked me.

"Go where?"

"I have something to show you."

I looked at Tex, who nodded.

"Sure," I said.

"Come this way."

Tsukino-san started back up.

I slowly stood and brushed the sand off my skin.

Tex rose too. He hunched a bit but still towered over me by a head.

I followed Tsukino-san but stopped when I saw that Tex wasn't coming after us. He hunched forward even more, his right hand on the left side of his rib cage.

"Are you okay?" I asked.

"Sometimes I get this sharp pain here, like a rope drawing tight around my chest." He patted where his hand rested on his ribs. "It comes and goes. You go with him."

I didn't see what I could do to help, so I turned and hurried as best I could to catch up with Tsukino-san. The sun floated free of the ocean. We walked on a long barrier where the lava tumbled into the ocean and formed a wall of rock. Below us, giant waves leapt against this wall, fell back, formed again, and rushed with violent velocity against the barrier. My soles burned on the rock and occasional patches of sand. At last we came to a peculiar formation, an indentation like a slide going down the rock wall and into the water.

Tsukino-san gestured for me to turn inland. I picked my way up the rock-strewn slope, following him to where he disappeared behind a large rock. There I found him looking down at a crudely built raft. It had no rudder, no sail, no place to escape the sun, no storage bin for supplies to survive an ocean journey. It looked like Tsukino-san and Tex had spent years collecting scrap from the beaches to make this craft of broken spars, planks, and logs. Lengths of rope and vine lashed the pieces into a whole about ten feet square.

"We are almost ready to go."

I didn't know what to say. To ride this raft into the waves promised a slow, certain death. It would bob like a cork, directionless, lost in the vastness of the ocean. No shipping lanes came near this island. If the raft managed to stay intact in the shark-infested waters, the currents might carry it almost anywhere.

"You want my help?"

"Yes. We've worked on this for many years. If we are to have any hope of success, we must launch the raft and begin our journey home."

I had an impulse to smile at the impossibility of what he proposed.

"How can I help?"

"Do you see what might improve it? You're young. You have the strength and energy to complete what we began. You can escape with us."

I compared the prospect of remaining on the island, living a life that was no life at all, with that of certain death on the ocean. It only took me a moment to decide.

"Fine," I answered, "let me think about what I can do."

That evening, as the sun began to set, Tsukino-san made a foray into the jungle on the other side of the island. Tex waved for me to come with him into the cave. He was still holding his ribs and moaning a bit with pain.

"What's wrong?" I asked.

"My heart," he answered. "It hurts."

"Take it easy," I said. "Maybe you should sit."

The cave was nothing more than a shaft of a dozen feet that widened to an oval at its end. In the fading light, I could see sand and leaves spread on the floor. On a wide ledge, like an altar, was a knife with a white handle and a straight blade, and two piles of small round stones. One pile was white and the other dark.

Panting, Tex squatted until his haunches touched the leaves and sand. He patted around him.

"Is this everything you have?" I asked.

"No, we have more. There are other caves. Tsukino-san likes to keep things neat. This is where we sleep."

"What are the stones for?"

"To play go. We make lines in the sand for a board."

"And the knife?"

"It's Tsukino-san's. Handed down in his family for generations. It has a name."

"Really?"

"Mayonaka."

I reached for the knife, the white handle cool in my palm. The blade looked sharp, and I let my thumb rest lightly on it.

"If you have the knife, why don't you escape?" I asked.

"I'm not healthy. And where would I go?"

"You could take the knife," I said, lifting it from the altar, "and make him your prisoner."

Tex looked up at me before replying.

"Would that be any better?" he asked.

"Of course," I answered. "Don't you think so?"

Tex slowly shook his head. "I don't see why it would be better. If he was crooked like a snake with cramps, well then I could understand. But he's as good an old boy as I am. If one of us has to be the prisoner, it may as well be me."

I knelt to level my eyes with his, but I saw no sign of doubt or wavering.

"How long have you worked on the raft?" I asked.

"We started almost as soon as I came here."

"It couldn't have taken that long to build. Why didn't you put it in the water a long time ago?"

"It was hard to finish."

"Why? Were you waiting for better materials?"

"No, not really." He rested his back against the wall of the cave.

"What, then?"

Tex reached toward me with his large hand. Touching his finger to the blade of the knife, he said, "Mayonaka means 'doom at midnight.'"

"It's a beautiful name, but not a pleasant meaning."

Tex took the knife from me and rested the handle in his palm.

"No, the meaning is beautiful too."

"Why?"

"Tsukino-san's ancestors were samurai who lived by a code of honor. If a samurai's lord ordered him to commit ritual suicide, seppuku, the samurai had to obey without a backward glance or regret. Only by doing so could he keep his honor. A blade like Mayonaka would be used to cut across the stomach. Then another person would use a larger sword to cut off the head."

"I don't see any beauty in that."

Tex raised a hand to quiet me.

"Mayonaka is a special knife. The samurai who carried it believed in the midnight light. In that sacred light, the samurai would have a vision of how precious life is. Whenever there was a reason to commit seppuku, the samurai, instead of blindly following the code of honor, would climb to a mountaintop at midnight to see the sacred light with its power to cure. From that high place, he would have a vision of what his life might be. It gave him the courage to value life. He would find hope. Doom would be the surrender of that hope."

"Surely," I said, "many of them must have committed seppuku anyway, even after waiting until midnight on a mountaintop."

"If a samurai found hope in life and its possibilities, at least he made a choice."

I didn't know what to say about such a choice and returned to where I'd been before this digression.

"So you don't care about being his prisoner?"

"I wouldn't say that," Tex answered patiently, "but taking him as my prisoner wouldn't make our lives any better."

"If we're lucky," I said, wanting to believe my words, "we'll be rescued once we launch that raft. Then it won't matter whether Tsukino-san thinks you're his prisoner. We can get you to a hospital. There are amazing operations now for the heart, tubes that open inside your blood vessels to keep the blood flowing and even bypass operations to give the heart new strength."

"You think the raft has a chance?" he asked.

"Why not? I'll make some improvements so it's more seaworthy. Then we'll be ready to go."

He nodded, a deliberate up and down, as if confirming some inner conclusion.

"That will be fine. You should make the improvements as soon as you can."

"After all the time you've worked on it, it won't seem very long."

Tex had been holding Mayonaka by the blade and tapping the white handle against his other palm.

"I should probably explain to you why it took us so long," he said. "Especially if you're going with us. You should know."

"Okay."

"Tsukino-san and I don't think that the raft has a chance. No matter how you improve it. It's just not good enough. If it doesn't capsize, it will drift. Anyone on it is as good as dead. That's one reason we didn't want to finish it."

"That seems like reason enough," I said, since this echoed my own thoughts. "Then why consider going out on it now?"

"There's another . . . thing." Tex chose the word after a moment of deliberation.

"What?"

"We agreed to something early on. Once we agreed, we felt that we would have no choice but to do what we had said. It was a sensible thing, for survival. But it's what made us keep finding faults with the raft. We would build it and take it apart. We kept constructing it in different ways. None of the rafts was that different, but we didn't want to finish."

"This agreement," I asked, shifting on the leaves and sand, "what was it?"

Tex raised Mayonaka, holding it vertically and focusing on the blade.

"That out on the raft, if we were still alive after we had used up the supplies, I would let Tsukino-san cut my veins with this knife. I would let him drink my blood. When I couldn't live any longer, I would let him kill me and eat my flesh. That is what we agreed."

"That's madness! Because you're his prisoner?"

"No."

"But . . ." I hardly knew where to begin with my objections. "That would be murder. If it won't work anyway, why leave the island?"

"Because we haven't much time left. If I die before the raft is launched, Tsukino-san will lose his best chance to survive."

"But you've been hiding from planes and boats for decades. Why go looking for people now?"

"I told you," Tex said. "I'm not well. We have to leave soon."

"And you want my help?"

"Yes. I want your help. Tsukino-san wants to visit the shrine for those who died in the wars. He wants to go back to his hometown and honor his parents' graves. I want him to get to Japan. And you, New York, I want you to get back to where you come from." As he spoke, his eyes began to shine. "I was born in Brownfield, south of Lubbock. I wouldn't mind going back, but I'll have to be satisfied wherever I end up. And if push comes to shove on the raft, I want you to share with Tsukino-san. Whatever I have to give, you share with him."

"But . . . ," I started to protest.

He waved a hand to silence me.

"It's what I want. And do me a favor." His mouth curled in a smile. "I always hoped to go to the top of the Empire State Building. See the skyline of the greatest city—that would be something. Next time you're up there, will you take a look for me?"

27

I heard the plashing of water. Turning on my light I saw the rocky shore of an underground lake. The water lay still and black as oil. I had no idea how deep it was or how far the lake might extend. Yet I had to continue, even if I swam to the far shore.

The sound came nearer until I saw a small boat with an oarsman standing at its stern.

"Give me one guilder. I'll take you to a good place." The boatman had a booming, cheerful voice. "Give me two, and I'll take you to a better one."

He laughed, a large man of sixty or so with matted hair, torn layers of loose clothes, a red bulbous nose, and a face streaked black with grime. He looked to be a bum, and a drunken one at that, judging by his boisterous voice and laughter. The boat entered an inlet near me and halted a few feet from the shore.

"What place?" I asked suspiciously

"Where the dogs are," he answered.

"Dogs?"

"You can't hear them now, but you will on the other side."

"What kind of dogs? Are they dangerous?"

"Guard dogs. Dangerous if you go where you shouldn't."

"What do they guard?"

"Questions, questions," he sang the words. "Are you coming with me or not?"

"Once I get over there"—I gestured with my head, and the miner's light flashed upward for a moment before returning to his face—"how will I return?"

"You pay for a round-trip."

"How do I know you'll be there?"

"I'm always here, on one side or the other. It's back and forth, back and forth. You'd think it would get monotonous, but I like helping people out." Here he stopped and, confirming my suspicions, drew a dark bottle from inside his tattered coat, unscrewed the top, and took a long drink. Clearing his throat happily, he twisted on the top and returned the bottle to his inner pocket. "Amazing how many people come here, like you, desperate to get to the other side. Don't have any idea what's over there. So tell me, if you don't know what's over there, why do you want to go?"

"I have to."

This made him reach into his coat, remove the bottle again, and imbibe.

"Want some?" he asked.

"No, no thanks."

"Up to you." He wiped his lips with the back of his coat sleeve and put the bottle away. "So, are we going or not?"

I looked at the black water and thought of the dogs.

"Yes, let's go."

The boat was still a few feet from the shore, but he didn't move to come closer.

"Judging by your underwear and boots, you must have been a fine-dressed gent, but I don't offer credit here. Unless you'd like to give me that nice light on your head as a guaranty for future payment."

"You want money?" I asked.

"Didn't I say as much?"

I reached under my tongue and brought out a silver coin. Holding it up, I saw that it appeared ancient, perhaps Greek, with a chariot and warriors led by a flying divinity on one side and a circular snake whose mouth engulfed its tail on the other. He paddled to the shore so I could hand it to him.

He examined the coin closely on each side, testing it between his teeth before pocketing it.

"All right, climb aboard."

"Both ways?"

"Yeah."

I crouched in the bow as he wove the oar back and forth to move us over the dark surface.

"So what brings you down here?" he asked.

I had turned off my light. He didn't have a lantern but seemed quite comfortable moving through the dark. Occasionally I would turn on the light and glimpse him standing in the stern, but I had to save the batteries.

"I'm not sure yet," I answered.

"Just a little excursion," he suggested in his cheerful way.

"You might say that."

"Leave anybody at home? A wife? A baby girl? A little guy named Junior?"

"No, no one."

I could hear the oar wagging from side to side.

"Why not?"

"I'm not married, for one thing."

"You're not that ugly, so why not?"

"I was married, but not anymore."

"Any regrets?"

"I don't know."

"Somebody steal her from you?"

"No, that's not what happened."

"Imagine this," he said. "A man comes to rob you. He comes at night and you're asleep. He has plenty of time to wander through your home. He uses his flashlight to find the gold and jewels you've hidden away."

"I don't have anything like that."

"He's persistent. Whatever you value, he eventually finds it. But when you wake in the dark and happen to stumble on him as you head for the toilet, what is he stealing?"

"I don't know."

"When you hear him, you go back for the pistol you keep in the side table by your bed. It's loaded. The safety is off. You face him, the pistol raised toward his chest. You're not ten feet away. At this range you couldn't miss. He has a large bundle over his shoulder, a plastic bag filled to bursting. He puts it on the floor and opens the top so you can see into it. It's filled with your trash, every bit of trash that he could find in the house. He's looking at you, waiting for you to decide. So what will it be?"

"I don't keep a pistol in the side table. I don't own a pistol."

"But imagine you did."

"I'm not going to shoot him. I don't care what he's stealing."

"Oh?"

"I told you. How much longer is it anyway?"

"We'll be there soon enough. But what if you confront the man and he has a bundle in his arms? As you look at him, you realize that the bundle is your baby, your newborn. He's kidnapping your child. You have the pistol and a clear shot at his head. Or, if you don't want to kill him, you can cripple him with a shot to the leg."

"I don't know."

"He has your child. What choice do you have?"

"Are you always so talkative?" I asked him.

"If you don't like pistols, how about this? A man wants to buy something and offers the price to the seller. What do you think the seller says?"

"I'll wrap it up for you," I answered, mystified at what he might be after.

"Maybe. Or maybe the seller says it's too much trouble to wrap it up. It's too much trouble to put it in a bag. In fact, it's too much trouble to sell it at all. So he tells the buyer to keep his filthy money. It's a matter of principle."

"I don't see it," I said.

"It has to do with the stars."

I looked up but saw only blackness above me.

"What are you talking about?"

There was a pause in the rhythm of the oar. Flicking on my light, I saw him take a long swallow from his bottle.

"You can learn so much from the stars—the patterns, the shifting of the planets."

"Yes?" I said dubiously as darkness returned.

"Marry when you have the chance, the sooner the better."

"If I meet the right person . . . ," I began.

"Because your time to be a father . . . it's passing. Maybe you have ten years. Yes, ten years at most. After that, it's a solo trip."

"How can you know that?"

"Do you like pie?" he asked.

"What are you talking about?" I yelled.

"Pi, the number. It should be perfect. If I had to choose a perfect shape, I would choose a circle. So why is the circumference divided by the diameter irrational? It makes no sense. It should be a golden number. Instead it runs off into eternity."

"What's your point?"

The hull of the boat scraped in the shallows. I clicked on my light. This shore looked as forbidding as the one we'd left behind. Jagged boulders thrust up in the darkness. He used his oar to hold the boat against a flat rock, and I stepped ashore.

"So it's good-bye, then," he said, pushing off a few feet.

"Until you take me back," I answered.

"Yes, of course." He bent and picked up a package from the bottom of the boat. "Take this. You may need it."

"For what?"

"You'll know," he replied, tossing it to land beside me.

I doubted whether he would come back.

"You'll be watching for me, won't you?"

"Yes, yes." He had slipped beyond the range of my light. I could hear the paddle and his final words. "When I bring you back, maybe you'll come for a visit with the missus and the little ones. Eat home-cooked food and sleep in a soft bed. Think it over."

28

Each day I sat in a shaded niche in the boulders and let my gaze shift back and forth from the poorly made square of the raft to the waves. Even on a calm day, I kept picturing the raft broken, capsized. I would see Tex, Tsukino-san, and myself sinking through the vast volumes of salt water to the distant bottom.

In another scenario, far worse than the first, the raft remained afloat. After a week or more adrift beneath the burning sun, we would have to deal with Tex. Would we really butcher him? I could refuse, couldn't I? But could I trust myself? Did I know to what lengths hunger and thirst might drive me?

Life on the island had to be better than facing such a quandary. Yet the island offered so little. Is it better to die on this barren outcrop? I had read enough of adventures on the high seas to know the unwritten law. If necessary for survival, human flesh could be consumed. Yet that law applied to shipwrecks, accidents, unforeseen tragedy, not premeditated murder. We could, after all, remain safely on land.

Tsukino-san visited often to sit with me for an hour or two. Small, wiry, browned by his years in the sun, he moved through the sweltering air with an ease that astonished me. He thought nothing of coming around midday, when the heat made the air tremble. He too had thoughts about how to improve the raft. One by one we discussed our ideas. I wanted us to be in agreement before we started the actual work. It wasn't until the fifth or sixth day that he inquired about something other than the raft.

"Were you married?" he asked.

I considered his question. It seemed so long ago.

"Yes," I answered.

He didn't ask another question that day. We began to dismantle the raft. We'd started early in the morning, before the fiery warmth of midday. The sun rose above the volcano's peak and cast its pink iridescence over the waves and the clouds in their hovering formations. We worked in a spot between two boulders that was shaded except during the middle of the day, when we'd break for several hours.

"Were you happy in your marriage?" he asked the next day as we finished unfastening the raft and began to rearrange its materials in a new shape. It would have a crude prow, a rudder, and, centered between them, a mast with a sail stabilized by a horizontal boom. This would give us some hope of moving with the winds and setting a course. It would be more difficult to construct, and require additional materials, but I believed that we could complete it within a week or ten days. Our first task was to set up log rollers so we could easily move it down the slope to the rocky embankment and slide it into the waves.

"Yes, for a time."

"Only for a time?" he asked, straining to roll a tree trunk into position.

I went to help him.

"We divorced."

He grunted. We pushed together and soon had the rollers in place so we could begin the raft itself.

"She disobeyed you?"

I wasn't certain how to respond to this.

"No, not at all," I finally replied.

"Why didn't you want her?" he asked.

"I did want her. We were married for ten years. In the end, she didn't want me."

His lips pursed in disgust, as if he had eaten something bitter.

"She lived in your household," he asserted. "Didn't your mother instruct her?"

"My mother didn't live with us. We lived by ourselves."

We worked in silence for a while. I knew he came from another culture and another time. He didn't ask more until we stopped at midday and moved deeper into the rocks to rest in the shadows.

"You had sex with your wife?"

"Yes."

"You enjoyed it?"

"Yes, very much."

"You did it often?"

"Yes."

"For ten years?"

"Yes, for ten years."

Tsukino-san sat with his legs crossed and his back erect like a monk in meditation. He closed his eyes. At first he'd seemed suspicious and quick to take offense, but he let go as we worked together. I could see the boy in this old man, a boy who had spent most of his life as far from the centers of civilization as one could imagine. I rested on my back, the humidity like a saturated cloth spread over my face.

"Did you have a son?"

I had fallen asleep. Often we napped and woke when the sun had moved behind the cliffs. He sat in the same posture. I raised myself on an elbow and pushed up to face him. The sleepiness remained with me. For a moment I was at a loss for how to answer.

"No."

"A daughter?"

"No."

"Could she have children?"

"Yes, I think so."

We returned to our work. For the most part I focused on what we had to do and not on the journey we would attempt.

Much later that day, when the sun hovered over the scarlet rim of the ocean, Tsukino-san asked me another question.

"Did you have a job?"

"Yes."

I expected him to ask what kind of job, but he didn't. We had begun to position the logs we would fasten together for the deck. Stopping for the day, we took the short walk back to the cave. Tex sat by the entrance, his back against the stone. He grinned and raised a hand when he saw us coming.

"How'd it go?" he asked.

"Fine," I answered.

"How much longer?"

Tired from my labor, I sat beside him.

"Maybe a week, give or take a few days."

"That'll be good. The sooner the better."

He said something like this every night when we came back. He wasn't well enough to walk the short distance and check on our progress for himself. His face had a pallid cast despite his deep tan, and he kept his hand pressed to the ribs on the left side of his chest.

"How are you doing?" I asked.

"To tell you the truth, I don't know."

"You feel worse?"

He shook his head. "It's about the same. I just want to make it on that raft."

"What is it, then?"

"Now that I can't move around much, all I do is think and daydream."

"What are you daydreaming about?"

"It's never one thing, but part of it's not very pleasant."

"Tell me about it."

"Today, about the war, the training, my buddies, the planes, some of the missions, and being shot down. I go over that again and again. Places I went that I had never heard of when growing up in Brownfield. Then," he gave a bashful smile, "about girls, the girls I knew back in high school mainly. I see them like they're standing in front of me. Sometimes I think I even smell them. And my mom. I remember her hugging me good-bye in the mornings before school. I'd grown too big to want her to kiss me, but she kissed me anyway. Every day. I'd hug her now if I could, you can bet on that. And working on the farm with my dad, the cattle, the fields, the pens. My mom cried when I enlisted. She hugged me and wouldn't let me go. My dad shook my hand and looked into my eyes. That's stayed with me always, that look. Today I got to thinking about where they're buried. I've thought about it before, but it was strong today. There's only one cemetery where they'd want to rest. It's in Brownfield. The entrance has brick pillars. Then it's flat, with grass that gets scorched and a bunch of trees that don't give enough shade. I imagined tramping through the old markers till I found my mom and dad side by side."

"Not the happiest thoughts," I said.

"That was the good part."

"What was the bad part?"

"Well . . . " Tex looked down and cleared his throat, his Adam's apple bobbing up and down. "I hardly know if I ought to say this, but somehow I want to. You know the way daydreams can be."

"Yes?"

"Well, the cave is pitch black at night, but we know how to find things in the dark. While you sleep, I reach up on the ledge and take Tsukino-san's knife. Then I rest my hand on your chest."

"In the dream," I said, not liking how easily this might have actually happened.

"I feel your heart beating, throbbing against my palm. There's a place where a knife can slip through the ribs and right into the heart. I hold the knife over that place and wait. I hear your breath going in and out. I hear Tsukino-san's breathing too, just a little distance from us. You know how dark the cave is. I can't see at all, just feel and hear. I smell sulfur. Taste it in my mouth. It's coming off the volcano or leaking out of the rock walls. I don't have a thought in my mind. Then I press the knife down. I hear a little sound, like a pop, then gurgling. I don't know if you bleed a lot. I run outside. I want to launch the raft and get away from here without you or him."

I couldn't answer when he finished. Tex seemed such a gentle man, but was this fantasy a warning?

"I told you it was pretty bad," Tex observed when I didn't say anything. "I should have kept my big trap shut."

"Why would you have a fantasy like that?" I asked.

"How should I know?" Tex answered. "Dreams have a mind of their own."

"I'm willing to stop working on the raft," I said.

"I know."

Tex didn't meet my eyes. He looked at the sand and brushed his free hand aimlessly back and forth.

"If that's what you want, you only have to say the word."

I was as willing to stop as I was to continue. I found it curious that I didn't feel more strongly either way. I wanted to join them in a community of shared interests and hopes. If they wanted to leave, then I wanted to help them. If they wanted to stay, then I would stay and never have to condone taking Tex's life on the high seas.

"No," he finally answered, "I want you to finish that raft as quickly as you can."

"You're sure?"

He looked up at me.

"As sure as I've been about anything."

Tex's daydream made me work even harder during the days that followed. I wanted to leave the island as soon as possible. Tex remained friendly, but I worried about the emotions he might be concealing from me and perhaps even from himself. I convinced Tsukino-san to leave his samurai knife at the raft so it would always be available for our work. It made me feel safer.

The raft slowly took on the shape we had imagined. It had a prow and a mast. Since we had no navigational instruments, we would rely on the position of the sun and the stars to set our course. We built up the raft's outer edges so they would extend down below the waterline as a precaution against capsizing and be high enough to keep out the waves. Whatever fresh water and other supplies we took, such as our rudimentary tools and scraps of clothing to protect us from the sun, would be covered with branches and tied to the deck to keep them from washing away in heavy seas. Life preservers frequently washed ashore. We left three loose, to take on deck, and lashed the rest to the outside of the raft for floatation.

From time to time, Tsukino-san returned to his leisurely cross-examination.

"Did you live in a house?"

"As a child. Now I live in a building in the city."

"A building," he repeated as if inhaling the scent of a rare blossom.

To my surprise, Tsukino-san brought out the parachute that saved Tex's life more than sixty years before. The thick fabric was stiff and hard to shape, but in the sand we made a pattern for the sail and used the samurai blade to cut what we needed. Then we trimmed strips to fasten it to the mast and the boom. It was makeshift, but we did our best with what we had at hand. In a storm we would be able to untie the sail from the boom and fasten the fabric around the mast.

"Did you have running water?" Tsukino-san asked when we finished attaching the sail.

"Yes."

"A bathroom?"

"Yes," I answered.

"Did it have a bathtub?"

He had stopped working and leaned against the side of a boulder.

"Yes, it did."

"Electricity?" he asked.

"Yes."

"Gas?"

"For cooking on the stove."

"And heat. Did you use wood?"

"No, oil. It heated the whole building."

I finished tying the thick strips of cloth in place and looked up to find Tsukino-san in a reverie. His dark eyes looked through me to somewhere in the distance.

"What a glorious life," he said at last, focusing his gaze on me. "How you must miss it."

29

I heard the dogs. Their howling seemed to rise from every direction as it bounced off the rocks. A shiver fluttered up my spine. I carried the package wrapped in paper in my right hand. Soon the headlamp dimmed ever so slightly. I shut it off. Whether I closed my eyes or kept them open, I was picking my way forward in the same utter darkness. I would carefully put a foot down to test the ground while moving my right hand in front of me to make certain nothing blocked my path.

I stopped as my hand touched a smooth surface. I flicked on my light and saw a tall doorway made of white marble. Immediately beside it another white doorway stood framed in the black rock. The howling of the dogs came closer.

I pushed the door on my left. Light blinded me as I stepped through it. I threw my arm over my eyes and only very gradually adjusted to the brightness. Above me was a vast expanse of white, like the skin of an albino. It was not sky. There was no sun. On the ground in front of me, lit by this light that had no discernable source, I saw burial markers.

I had once been to Normandy and seen the cemeteries for the soldiers. The white crosses went on and on in rows as neat as strong, young men aligned in a vast formation. Here, before me, was a cemetery reminiscent of that, except that each grave had a marble headstone. Still dazed by the brightness of the light, I wandered on the lawn among the headstones. After a while I stopped here and there to read an inscription, but most of the stones were written in languages I didn't know. I could identify French, Spanish, Italian, even Latin and Greek. And I could at least guess at the countries represented by Cyrillic and other characters. But there were other markings—like hiero-glyphs, runes, and even stranger symbols—of which I could make nothing.

I tried to understand the reason for this vast cemetery. Who had created it? Why bring together remains, not only from every region of the world but also, as the inscriptions indicated, from vastly different times?

I walked on and on until I realized that this burial ground must have no boundaries. I might walk forever and never come to where the headstones ended. The grass was perfectly mani-cured, like a putting green or the infield of a major-league baseball stadium. Perhaps every thousandth headstone had an inscription in English. I lingered over these. The first one simply said, "The Lord gave and the Lord hath taken away. Blessed be the name of the Lord."

I moved on and found another that said, "Thy will be done." When I read the entire inscription, I saw that this little girl had died in the third year of the Civil War. I could feel the grief of her parents in the brief epitaph and the careful record of her age—two years, two months, and eleven days. But, I thought, even if she had lived a full life span, she would have died long ago.

Another inscription said, "Sacred to the memory of my mother. As a wife devoted, as a mother affectionate, as a friend ever kind and true."

"'Tis not the whole of life to live, nor all of death to die," I read while kneeling in front of another headstone, and the next one I found said, "Each lonely scene shall thee restore."

"To know him was to love him," wrote a wife.

A husband said, "To live in hearts we leave behind is not to die."

Tired at last, I sat facing a headstone on which the epitaph read, "Music, when soft voices die, vibrates in the memory." I felt something vibrate in my memory. I had come here to find something or someone. Why no image shaped in my mind, telling me what or who, I don't know. If I looked at a thousand headstones, I might see a name that would waken me to my purpose. I rose and moved among the tombstones more quickly. If I found a familiar name, the right name, I might know why I had been compelled to come here at all. I walked farther and farther, looking left and right for names that might spark my memory. Finding none, I began to run along the rows. When I could run no more, my face wet with sweat or tears, I knew I couldn't stay any longer. Carefully I began to retrace my steps.

Several times I feared I had lost my way, but at last I pushed against the door and returned to the darkness on its other side.

Now I opened the door on the right. The same light flooded over me, and I shaded my eyes. I could see no difference in the long rows and columns of headstones that, as in the first cemetery, filled the landscape, seemingly without end. I sighed and shifted my package from one arm to the other. I looked for headstones with inscriptions in English. Everything about this cemetery suggested that it was identical to the first.

The first headstone in English showed me my mistake. There was a name and a date of birth, but no date of death. It had to be an oversight. I walked farther, but even the headstones in foreign languages showed only dates of birth. There were no inscriptions, no epitaphs. Studying the birth dates, I realized that all of them were relatively recent. Because no date of death appeared, I could only assume these people were living. If I searched far enough, I would find headstones for myself and everyone I knew.

Fatigue sapped me. Though only a short distance from the entry, I didn't know if I could return to the marble door. Slowly I placed one foot after another, like a man in a storm leaning forward against the violent shove of the wind. When the door slammed behind me, I collapsed in an exhausted stupor.

I woke to the sound of chewing, interrupted by snatches of conversation.

"He's coming around," said a shrill voice.

"How are you, my friend?" asked a deeper voice.

"Who are you?" I replied, struggling to move my arm and turn on my light.

"Thanks for the meat," said a voice in between the other two.

"Yes, thanks."

I finally managed to flick the switch. At first I imagined I saw a dog with three heads—a dachshund's, a golden retriever's, and a German shepherd's. But my vision steadied, and I realized that their heads were only close together over the torn paper of the package I'd been carrying. I could see their separate bodies as they tore at the red meat.

"This is very good," said the golden retriever. "It reminds me of the delicacies that turned up outside a butcher shop I used to frequent. How I looked forward to pawing through those trash cans."

"Are you all right?" asked the German shepherd in his deep voice. "You look as if you've had a shock."

"Do you know what's behind these doors?" I asked, gesturing toward them.

"You weren't supposed to get in," said the shrill dachshund. "What are you doing here anyway?"

"I can't remember the last time somebody came," said the retriever with his mellow voice. "So we're not always here. We like to get exercise, go for a run."

"You were supposed to keep me out?"

The German shepherd nodded, and all three of them looked abashed.

"Why doesn't one of you guard the doors while the other two run?" I asked.

"It's more fun if we all go," said the retriever.

"It's just better," agreed the dachshund.

"But . . . ," I started to protest.

"How can we help you?" asked the German shepherd.

The dachshund stretched, his small front paws extended and his spine curving from low between his shoulders to where his brown rump reached upward. "I'm getting sleepy."

"What's up ahead?" I asked.

"You don't really want to know." The German shepherd punctuated his response with a large yawn.

"I'm going there anyway."

He shook his head. "We can't allow that."

"But why?"

"It's for your own good."

"Let me decide what's for my own good," I answered sharply.

"You can't go," he answered, and yawned again.

"Are you sleepy?" asked the dachshund.

"Yes," said the golden retriever.

"I am too," agreed the German shepherd.

"This happened before," said the retriever, "quite a while ago. Remember?"

"You're right," said the dachshund. "We ate and then we had to sleep. We simply couldn't stay awake."

The dachshund closed his eyes, and the German shepherd kept showing his long teeth as he yawned ever more widely.

"It's such an effort to stay awake," he said as the retriever lay down to sleep beside the dachshund. "Look, I can't stop you, but I'm asking you not to go forward."

"I have to go," I repeated, feeling the compulsion that had brought me this far.

"Listen to me. You don't know what you're getting into."

"Will you be all right?" I asked, concerned to see him getting groggy like the others.

"We'll be fine. It's you I'm concerned about."

"I'm sorry about the meat," I said.

"You won't reconsider?"

"No," I answered.

"Maybe," he said, his eyes fluttering in his efforts to keep them open, "it will all work out for the best."

"But why would you want to stop me?" I asked.

"You'll see. She's in her kitchen. That's where we went on our last run."

"Is it straight ahead?" I asked.

"You can't miss it. All the paths end there. Take care, my friend," he said with a sad glistening in his dark eyes. He walked a few times in a circle and at last curled up to sleep beside his comrades.

30

"Did you parachute from a plane?" I asked Tsukino-san one evening as we tidied up the work site. His suspicions about my being a spy made me hesitant to ask questions like this.

"No," he answered, placing scraps of wood in piles.

The glow of sunset tossed a scarlet wash over the long striations of the horizontal clouds. The raft was nearly complete. Crude, yes, but far better than before. The mast lifted skyward. The rudder could be fit in place to move the pointed prow this way or that.

"How did you come here?" I asked.

"Underwater."

"By submarine?"

He shook his head.

I smiled because he had to be joking with me. I would have called him Jonah, but he probably hadn't read the Bible.

"How then?"

"A *kaiten*."

"A what?"

"A torpedo."

"You came in a torpedo?"

"Yes, in 1944 our navy modified large torpedoes so they could be piloted. I volunteered to protect Japan from invasion."

"I never heard of this," I said, not sure if he was telling me the truth.

"It was necessary."

He spoke matter-of-factly. If young pilots had been willing to die for their country, why not men in the navy?

"You volunteered to die?"

"I was willing to do whatever was necessary for my country."

"Didn't you care about your life?"

Tsukino-san smiled, or perhaps he grimaced.

"When I volunteered, I said good-bye to the life I had hoped to live. Later, as I trained, I felt great sorrow to be leaving my parents. Each night we drank sake together, hundreds of young men in uniform. We wrote poems about cherry blossoms and recited them. How brief is that beautiful moment of the blossoms—that is what all the poems said. Then we sang songs and drank more sake." He gestured to the island. "There are no cherry trees here. I haven't seen their blossoms in such a long time."

"You didn't want to die?" I always thought the pilots eager to kill themselves.

"No one wanted to die."

"But your mission was certain death."

"No."

"To ride a torpedo into a ship?"

"If it were certain death, I would be dead."

"Why aren't you?"

We had settled on the rim of the raft as we talked.

"The *kaiten* could go at," he paused to calculate, "forty knots and had a three-thousand-pound warhead. They were small enough to slip through submarine nets and get into harbors. The first group of *kaiten* engaged the enemy in November 1944, at the Ulithi Atoll. Eight *kaiten* sank three carriers and two battleships. This great victory encouraged us, and my mission came soon after. We had one submarine with four *kaiten* held on the deck by cables. When we found the enemy, I squeezed into the pilot's tiny chamber. There was a periscope. Look . . . "

He pointed to a scar on his cheek.

"How did that happen?" I asked.

"While training. It was such a small space. Many of us were cut by the periscope. The controls were rudimentary—just enough to steer into the hull of the target. I turned toward a destroyer, increasing my speed to the maximum."

"What did you feel?" I asked.

"I no longer had human concerns. I had escaped the accidents of life. Illness and old age meant nothing to me. In the moment of my passing, a great service would be done. I had been called and I had answered to the navy, the nation, and the emperor."

"No regrets?"

"Not then."

"You didn't hit the destroyer," I said.

"I did. I hit it right in the center."

I opened my hands to express my perplexity at how he could have survived.

"I was knocked out," he said. "When I came back to my senses, the *kaiten* was no longer moving. I tried to look through the periscope, but it had been destroyed. I wanted to unscrew the hatch, but I was certain the *kaiten* had come to rest on the ocean's bottom. If the hatch stuck, I would suffocate. If I could unscrew it, I would drown. I waited in the darkness, breathing the last of the oxygen. I began to feel faint. At last I placed my hands on the wheel to turn the hatch. It moved, and soon I saw daylight. Squeezing out, I realized the *kaiten* had run aground on a sandbar. I swam to the beach. I've been here ever since."

"When the *kaiten* hit the hull . . . ," I began to ask.

"It didn't explode. The warhead must have been defective. Because I approached at an angle, the *kaiten* may have glanced off the hull and continued."

We sat in silence. All three of us had come to this island because the marvel of a modern machine had failed, leaving us to live by our hands and wits.

"Where is the *kaiten* now?" I asked.

Tsukino-san pointed to the waves.

"For a long time it was over in that direction, but typhoons have come and gone. The sandbar shifted. The *kaiten* slipped away. Even if we could find it, there's nothing we could use in it."

I hadn't been thinking of salvage. Somewhere on the ocean's bottom was the *kaiten* with its defective warhead, its damaged periscope, and its open hatch.

"Tomorrow we'll load the supplies and go," I said, waiting for confirmation from Tsukino-san.

He rose and looked for some time at the raft and its path to the ocean.

"Yes," he agreed.

"Is everything okay?" I asked.

He seemed reluctant, perhaps of two minds about our departure. If he felt that way, I could certainly understand.

"Yes."

"Shall we see how Tex is doing?" I asked.

"Yes, let's go back."

That night we sat on the sand in front of the cave and talked for a long while. The excitement of leaving the next day made us laugh and ignore the growing force of the wind.

"Once," Tsukino-san said, "I called him Tex-san. Then he told me he was indeed a Texan."

"Hey, New York—san," Tex interjected.

"New Yorker," I corrected.

"What will you do when you're home?"

"Sleep on a mattress. With a pillow."

"Ambitious man," said Tsukino-san jokingly. Then turning serious, he continued, "I will go to the Yasukuni Shrine for those who fell in the wars. To give my respects and my thanks. I will say a thousand prayers."

After a moment of reflection, he looked at Tex. Their eyes met, and he added quietly, "After I pray for the men I knew and fought beside, I'll pray for all the dead. For yours and mine. Then I'll go home."

Tex didn't change his expression, but he was quiet.

"Bring your snow shovel," he finally said, his levity deflecting Tsukino-san's intensity.

"I grew up in the snow country," Tsukino-san explained.

"The houses have doors on the second story," Tex said.

"Yes, the snow can cover the first story. Inside the house, if you look out the windows, you only see a wall of snow. You have to light lanterns or it's as dark as night."

"It wasn't like that in Texas."

"I want to see the mountains again, snow on their peaks," Tsukino-san said. "I want to visit the graves of my mother and father."

We fell silent for a few moments. I wondered how Tex must feel, since he too dreamed of going to his parents' resting place. Or how he felt to hear Tsukino-san speak of what would happen in Japan. Nothing like that was likely be in Tex's future. And how long would Tsukino-san live in any case? Was his fate so much better than Tex's? At that moment, as happened from time to time, I thought about what might occur on the boat after Tex was gone. Having killed and devoured one man, what would stop either of us from killing another? Would I kill Tsukino-san or be his victim?

"Did you know that Tsukino-san writes poetry?" Tex asked.

"Still?" I asked, recalling what Tsukino-san said about the poetry he wrote while training.

"Yes. And I translate it," Tex said.

I found it easier to believe Tsukino-san wrote poetry than that Tex translated it.

"I give Tex some ideas and images," Tsukino-san said. "He puts the words together."

"Don't listen to him," Tex countered. "He's finished with them before I start. And they're a lot better in Japanese."

"I'd like to hear them."

"Okay, here goes," Tex said, and began a slow, heartfelt recitation:

Long ago I dreamt of what might be.
How I wish to be that dreamer again.
Melting snow
On the slopes of Mount Kirigamine.

"Kirigamine?" I questioned.

"It towers above the town of my birth," Tsukino-san said.

"Can you repeat the poem?"

Tex did and waited a few moments, then asked, "Ready for another?"

"Sure."

"This one needs a little explanation."

"Speak it first," Tsukino-san interposed.

Tex complied:

Mother, my mother,
A thousand stitches you gathered
To bring home
Your wandering son.

"My mother waited near the temple," Tsukino-san said, "and asked a thousand women to each sew one stitch on a *senninbari*."

"That's a sash," Tex offered. "It goes around the soldier's middle to protect him."

"The red stitches bring good luck," Tsukino-san went on, "and mine included the words 'eternal good luck in war.' I wore it under my uniform on the *kaiten*."

Tex continued with another:

On the seventh day
Of the seventh month
Ten thousand wings
Forge the bridge of love.

"Explain," Tsukino-san encouraged Tex.

"It's from a folktale. The Sky Emperor had a daughter named Orihime, who was a weaver. She met a herder of cows named Hikoboshi. Orihime and Hikoboshi fell in love at first sight, but they were so much in love that they neglected their duties. This angered Orihime's father, who separated them with the Milky Way. But Orihime wept so long and bitterly for her lover that her father relented. One night a year, on July 7, he allows kindhearted magpies to build a bridge across the Milky Way so the lovers can be together," Tex finished. "I was a cowherd too. Wish I'd been in love like that."

"One more," Tsukino-san broke in. "We'll go at dawn to load the raft. When we have it loaded, we'll come back for Tex."

"You don't have to get me," Tex protested. "I'm walking out of here on my own two feet."

"Don't be ridiculous," Tsukino-san admonished him. "You know we have a litter for you."

We had made the litter from two strong branches and a piece of the parachute. It had the shape of a triangle, and the pointed end dragged on the ground. Tex was bigger than Tsukino-san or me, so we couldn't simply carry him. It would be a bumpy ride for Tex, but we would only have to do it once.

Tsukino-san said something in Japanese.

"He wants you to hear this one," Tex said.

In the great-trunked tree
My father sits
Beside his father.
Wind over buds and branches.

After this last poem, we entered the cave for our final night on the island. Soon I fell into a deep sleep.

31

My nose quivered with the delicious odors of cooking. I followed these scents like clues in the darkness until I could go no farther. Turning my light back on, I saw a shining black door ahead of me. I hesitated a moment, then knocked.

"Come in," called a woman.

I stepped through the door into a kitchen like no other I've seen. It had giant refrigerators, large tables for food preparation, stoves with a dozen burners, and an oven with a door like the opening to a barn. As my eyes adapted to the light, I looked at the woman, who stood beside a rectangular table with a butcher-block top. It was Numun, the gemlike woman, with her rubious skin aglow. She wore a dress, cape, and hood of immaculate white. Covering much of the floor were large woven baskets shaped as cornucopias, which overflowed with corn, squash, yams, melons, beets, turnips, carrots, artichokes, and more. Before her, on the table, an equally white sheet covered a shape that might have been a body. In fact, seeing her this way, I imagined her like a priestess of some ancient cult.

"Are you hungry?" she asked. "This kitchen is so extensive that you can ask for almost anything. Perhaps a ragout of kangaroo tail or bird's nest soup?"

"What's that?" I interrupted.

"The nests are made from saliva of the cave swift. The soup aids digestion, alleviates asthma, and raises libido. Or you could have a steak of camel's hump, raw or roasted termites, maggot cheese ... "

"No no," I demurred.

"Ant stir-fry?" She raised her eyebrows with the question. "Take three hundred large, female red-bodied ants, add one tablespoon of vegetable oil and one medium-sized chopped onion. Heat the oil in a skillet, then stir-fry the onion and ants together until the onion is well browned."

I shook my head.

"Or locusts? The book of Leviticus allows the eating of locusts. In Mark and Matthew we're told that John the Baptist nourished himself on locusts and wild honey."

"I don't think so," I managed to interject.

"What a shame," she said. "Perhaps golden salamander en papillote? The recipe calls for fennel seeds, black peppercorns, powder of rhinoceros horn, coriander seed, red pepper flakes, bay leaves, oil of sperm whale, lemon slices ... "

She continued, but I was remembering walking by a stream as a child. One by one I turned over the flat rocks, curious about what lay beneath them. I saw worms, ants, grubs, centipedes, and tiny dark salamanders that scattered in fear. But under one rock I found the golden salamander of which she spoke. It was enormous in comparison to the others, three or four times as big, and on its golden skin were black dots. It didn't try to run but looked unblinkingly at me like a king who finds an intruder in his domain. I wanted ever so much to pick him up and take him with me, but something in his dark eyes deterred even my boyish enthusiasm. So I lowered the rock and restored him to the darkness he ruled.

"I'm not really hungry," I offered.

"Yes, you are," she contradicted me, moving closer. "You're afraid to eat what I offer you."

"No no."

"Salamanders are immortal." She stepped to within a hand's reach of me. "Eat, and become like them."

"They aren't immortal," I said, uneasy with her closeness.

"Yes, they certainly are."

"How do you know?"

"Because they cast no shadows."

I pictured that golden salamander. It was many years ago, but I didn't remember a shadow, just the dark intensity of its eyes.

"Anyway," I replied, "I really have no appetite."

"But you're my guest. Tell me what I can do to please you."

With this she stepped forward and touched the shells of my ears. I trembled as first she rubbed the tops and then the bottoms and the lobes. She was against me, her stomach pressing into me. Pleasure quivered in the base of my spine. It rose ever so slowly, vertebra by vertebra, like an exquisite flower lifting toward the ecstatic light pouring in through the openings of my eyes.

"Are you pregnant?" I gasped when I could speak again.

She had moved away from me and stood by the table. In her flowing garments, I couldn't be certain whether her abdomen rose in a mound.

"If I were, would you marry me?" she teased with a smile. "This kitchen is tiny compared to my house, which is filled with wealth and things of beauty. You can share all I have."

"I can't stay here."

"But your choices are limited," she replied.

"What do you mean?"

"You can either remain here or you can go back the way you came. Nothing more."

"But . . . " I'm not sure why, but I couldn't believe those were my only choices. The impulse that made me come all this way . . . I felt it still. I wanted to continue.

"Of course, each alternative has its nuances, its special attractions," she continued.

"What are they?"

"This is a large kitchen, very large. I could use help here. Perhaps you would like a job."

I had a recollection of once wanting employment of this kind. I frowned, but the details eluded me.

"What do you think?" she inquired when I failed to respond.

"What would my title be?" I asked to gain a little time.

"Sous-chef. You would oversee the transformation of raw vegetables and meats into edible and delicious foods. I know you have the training for it."

"You do?"

"From the CIA."

How could she know about my visit to the Culinary Institute of America?

"You have a knack with recipes, with the processes that change one thing into another."

"No, not sous-chef," I answered.

"Choose your title," she offered grandly, "and you have a place here."

"Thank you, but no."

"No?"

I didn't know what to expect. She turned to the massive oven, reached up to grasp its silver handle, and pulled open the door. Her white garments were silhouetted by the orange flames leaping inside that inferno. I came closer, expecting a searing blast of heat. But the flames had the quality of ice as well as fire. The immense oven had no floor, and the flames leapt above a column of magma that must have risen miles from the mantle of the earth.

"Here you can prepare your recipes." She encouraged me with a wave of her hand. "Won't you reconsider?"

I stared into this conflagration. Once I would have been delighted at such a job offer. But why should she care about my recipes?

"I have to keep going forward," I answered at last.

She shook her head.

"There is no forward from here," she said sharply, "only back."

Moving to the butcher-block table, she rested her hands on the sheet covering the form beneath it. I wanted to remain gazing into the depths of the magma, but I went to face her across the table.

"The question is whether you'll go back alone."

"What do you mean?"

"Take someone with you if you want."

"But who?"

"What about . . . "—with a dramatic sweep of her arms, she pulled back the sheet that covered the form on the table before her—". . . this man?"

I looked at the tall and slender body of a pale-skinned, elderly man clad in a loincloth. His eyes were closed as if in a peaceful dream. I felt a glimmer of recognition. Gently I placed my hand on his forehead, but he felt neither warm nor cold.

"Why is he here?" I asked her.

"He's between," she answered.

"Between what?" I waited for her to reply. When she said nothing, I haltingly added, "He was my mentor and . . . my friend."

"Here"—she gestured to the four walls of the kitchen— "he's in transition, unless you take him with you."

Slowly she lifted her open hand, and the body creased at the waist and rose like a cobra to the melody of a fakir's flute.

"Is he dead?" I asked.

"I told you," she answered, her gesture bringing him off the table and onto his feet. "He is between. If you choose, he will follow you wherever you go. Sunlight will waken him. Then, for a time, he will be as he was before."

"Only for a time?"

She gave a fleeting smile but didn't answer.

"And there is a condition."

"What?"

"Until the sunlight opens his eyes, you must not think of him as he used to be."

I considered this.

"And if I do think of how he was?"

"He will vanish."

"And go where?"

"You know the answer to that."

I thought of the first cemetery, with its innumerable head-stones.

"How can you hesitate?" she demanded as the aged body stood slackly beside her.

"No," I said.

"No?"

I repeated the word more loudly. In response, she raised an arm and pointed the body toward the open door of the oven. Without opening its eyes, the slender figure followed her direction. Step after step it advanced toward the flames. I wanted to cry or reach out as it paused at the mouth of the oven. Then it stepped forward and vanished in the flames and molten magma.

Turning around, I was shocked to see Numun lying on the butcher-block table. She rested on her back, her legs bent and her white gown pulled up around her waist. She wore no underclothing. Between her legs, in the opening of her vagina, I could see the crown of a baby's emerging head.

She caught my expression and laughed despite her exertions. Suddenly I connected the body that had vanished in the oven to this baby being born before me. In that moment I saw an option beyond staying here with her or returning in the darkness through which I had come.

Her laughter continued—laughter for all she knew that I would never know. She watched me as I moved and neared the oven door. Then, to the cascades of her wild laughter, I leapt to join my mentor in the salamandrine fires.

*T*he tide brought the waves crashing against the rock face below the raft. Despite the violence of that headlong rush, Tsukino-san and I loaded our craft. He and Tex had saved a motley of bottles that had washed ashore and filled them with fresh water gathered from noonday storms. By leaving containers of seawater in the sun until they evaporated and left only a crust of salt, they made brine to preserve the flesh of grubs, crabs, worms, mussels, clams, fish, and the occasional bird. They shaped stoppers of wood to seal the bottles. If rationed, this food and water would last for two weeks. Tsukino-san held Mayonaka in one hand, a naked man with a blade that reached from his hip nearly to his knee. I had expected him to wear the sash of a thousand stitches or the white headband that had adorned his forehead on his mission in the *kaiten*. But they, like his and Tex's uniforms, had long since fallen to pieces. Only the parachute had survived, and we'd use its remaining scraps on the raft to shelter us from the sun. Tsukino-san gestured with his head to show that it was time to return to the cave and use the litter to bring Tex to the raft.

I started up the path. Once Tex settled in the litter, it would take about twenty minutes, or a half an hour at most, to bring him to the launching site.

I was half a dozen steps ahead of Tsukino-san when I saw the body. I ran forward and dropped to my knees, holding my hand to Tex's wrist to feel for his pulse.

"You fool!" Tsukino-san cried out at the inert body, thrusting me aside.

He slapped Tex's cheeks, gently at first and then more forcefully.

"Wake up!" he yelled and placed his arms around Tex to pull him up to sitting. "Wake up!"

I didn't know what to do. Standing a few feet away, I watched Tsukino-san rock Tex's body ever more violently. When Tex didn't awaken, Tsukino-san at last became still. He held Tex's torso upright in his arms.

"He wanted to walk," I said, helpless in the face of what had happened.

Tsukino-san simply hugged Tex. I reached out to comfort Tsukino-san, but the raised muscles on his arms felt like stone. He paid no attention to me. I stepped away and sat with my head cradled in my hand. Tex didn't want a meaningless death like this. He had hoped to free Tsukino-san and me from our confinement on this island.

A high-pitched cry woke me from my misery. Tsukino-san had thrown back his head. The cry, strangled and inhuman, protested—refused to accept—this waste. Quickly Tsukino-san shifted to arrange himself with his legs crossed beneath him and his back straight. He took Mayonaka in both hands and pointed the blade toward his lower right abdomen.

"No, I'll take his place!" I yelled at him. "Let me take his place."

He sat no more than ten steps away from me. Tex's body separated us. But as my muscles tensed to move, he brought the knife into himself. For a moment, I believed he was uninjured. Then I saw how deeply the blade sunk, how close the handle came to his skin. The blood bubbled up like water from a spring. His two hands strained to move the blade across the depths of his stomach. I looked at his face, but he had flown from me. He turned the blade to gash upward. As he began to cut back across, his eyes rolled and his arms ceased their motion. Slowly he toppled to rest beside Tex.

I knelt in the bright pool of his blood.

"Why didn't you wait?" I raged, tears pouring down my cheeks.

One bloody index finger pointed. It surprised me, because I thought he was dead. He lifted the finger, though his hands were still wrapped around Mayonaka, and pointed toward his throat. I understood, but I did nothing. The finger uncurled a second time and pointed again. Would I let him die a slow, painful death? A third time the finger lifted, trembling, opening joint by joint. I pried open his hands and pulled Mayonaka free. Anchoring his head between my knees, and holding the blade in both my hands as he had done, I drove in the point and with all my strength moved the blade across his neck. Blood spurted on my face, chest, stomach, and arms. Wiping my eyes, I saw that I had nearly severed his head from his body. I slipped one hand beneath his head and the other between his shoulder blades and rolled him over so his head rested facedown on Tex's shoulder. Tex faced the sky.

Picking up Mayonaka, I stumbled toward the raft. If only Tex hadn't tried to walk that short distance. And why hadn't Tsukino-san accepted my offer to take Tex's place? I would have surrendered my life on the raft. I would have been the nourishment that sustained Tsukino-san on his long journey home. If he were going to take his own life, why hadn't he waited for the midnight light, the sacred light that would guide him?

Had I murdered Tsukino-san? Yes, I must have. I, who imagined that I wanted to injure no one, not even Tex who would have died anyway. I pulled the knife across arteries and veins and esophagus and windpipe. I should go back. I should return to that place where the old men embraced. If I didn't want to hollow a grave in the sand, I could certainly pile up stones to protect their bodies and mark their passing.

Instead I rushed on and pushed aside the rocks that anchored the raft. Holding onto the mast, I made the terrifying descent down the sloping cliff face and into the waves. I manned the sail and held the rudder. Slowly the island became smaller and smaller. At night the moon and stars hung like bright ornaments in the sky. I oriented myself and tried to remember the charts I had glanced at during my passage to the island. But I couldn't bring the prevailing currents and winds clearly to mind. My plan was merely to keep moving, always in the same direction.

Day after day I steered the raft in as close to a straight line as I could achieve. I watched for ships, but the island had been far from the shipping lanes. I wrapped myself in a cloak cut from the parachute. This gave me protection from the sun during the day and from the cool winds and ocean spray at night. Soon I realized how unfortunate a choice it had been to preserve the food in brine. The salt made my thirst unquenchable. Yet I had to drink as little water as I could. Without Tex and Tsukino-san, I calculated I might survive six weeks if I conserved the supplies. But each day I drank more water than planned. By the end of the second week, I had only enough left for another two weeks.

I fished with crude hooks we'd fashioned, and failed. I tried to net the gulls that landed on the raft, but I might as well have tried to harvest quicksilver. Far too agile to be caught by my clumsy lunges with the parachute fabric, the gulls would simply lift off the raft and float in the air only a few feet from me, as safe as if they'd been in the highest heavens.

At night I could see the constellations. The moon first waxed, until its silver dominated the firmament, and then waned. Occasionally rains would pour down, but the ocean remained calm, with swells of no more than four or five feet. When I slept, I would lash myself to the deck as a precaution. The rest of the time I simply moved the sail to catch the prevailing winds and kept the rudder firm. I tried to calculate how far I traveled as each day passed, but even though I had read of ancient Greeks who measured the circumference of the earth by using shadows, I could make no sensible calculations. I could only hope that I was moving toward the shipping lanes and populated islands.

I used Mayonaka to mark the passage of each day with a notch. On the afternoon of the twenty-third day, the sky ahead of me began to darken. First it turned gray at the horizon and I thought that there would simply be another downpour of rain, but the gray became black and grew in size until it curtained all I could see. I looked behind me and saw a faint glimmer of light. I considered turning and running for that tiny glow, but it might have taken days to go that far.

The waves grew in size. I strapped on a life preserver. Quickly I detached the sail from the boom and wrapped it around the mast. I checked the supplies to make sure they were fastened as tightly as possible. The empty containers I left upright in the hope of catching rainwater. I slipped Mayonaka within a hollowed section of a tree trunk I had fit to one side of the raft and forced a wooden plug I had fashioned into the opening to keep it safe. Then I squeezed into the right angle where the raft's side met the deck and did my best to bind myself to it with ropes and vines.

The waves rose higher and higher in frothing surges. Ten- and fifteen-foot swells tossed the raft. Rain came, lightly at first and then pelting the deck as the winds howled above. The waves enlarged to twenty and twenty-five feet. The raft bobbed like a cork, frightening ascents followed by sickening tumbles to the troughs. At last darkness as absolute as in the ocean's depths enveloped me. Soaking wet despite my cloth covering, I shivered uncontrollably.

Then, in one terrifying moment, the raft flipped end over end. When it struck the waves, I was beneath it. I choked on the salty water. The bonds that had held me safe now threatened me with drowning. Even if I could struggle free, what good would it do? If my life preserver buoyed me, I would be floating in the open ocean without food or water. Yet I would be alive. With that thought, I struggled to loosen my bindings. Then suddenly I could breathe, but only because the raft was flying through the darkness. It landed with crushing force, but I could inhale without swallowing salt water. This time it had landed upright, but the next wave or the wave after could easily flip it again and drown me.

At last the waves began to subside, the winds calmed, and the rain tapered to mist and vanished. The firmament reappeared as the dark clouds broke apart, and the slender crescent moon showed itself at the far side of the sky. Soon after, a dawn began like no other I have ever seen. It lit the waves, clouds, and sky with a rosy light so saturated and intense that it seemed to me a birth canal through which creation itself was replenished.

Carefully I calculated my losses. The mast, boom, and sail had vanished. A hole where the mast had been torn free let a foot of seawater cover the deck. The raft wouldn't sink, but I couldn't lie down. Worse, all the supplies had washed overboard. I had no more of the briny food and, more important, no water. At last I stopped cataloging my losses; it was simpler to enumerate what remained. I had the life preserver I was wearing, the cloak cut from the parachute, the ropes and vines that bound me to the deck. Opening the hollow where I secured Mayonaka, I saw that I still also possessed the samurai blade.

Sitting with my legs crossed in the sloshing water and my back supported by the side of the raft, I tried to organize my thoughts. I looked in every direction in the hope of sighting land. But I had been traveling so long that it seemed the continents had vanished and the oceans joined seamlessly to form an endless expanse in which I might float forever without making a landfall. For all I knew, civilization had vanished and the bonds that connected one human to another had disappeared.

At last I drowsed sitting straight up in water that reached my navel. When I opened my eyes, I saw Tex and Tsukino-san. I don't believe in ghosts, but I didn't know what else to call them. How could they be with me if I were still alive? I stared at them but didn't speak. Both were far younger than the men I'd known on the island. They were naked, and their skin had a fullness and hue that was hardly ghostly. They sat opposite me, perched on the far side of the raft. My age now, they looked to be far healthier than me. I had long since shed the roll of flesh around my middle and shrunk to an emaciated semblance of my original self.

"You're taking on water." Tex broke the silence. He had the same accent, the same ambling speech, like a tourist with time to linger over the most uninteresting sights.

"Yes," I answered, "but it's not sinking."

"You have to repair it," Tex said flatly.

"You don't understand," I replied. "The supplies are gone, the water. I have a few more days, but I'm not going to make it."

"That's not for you to say," Tsukino-san broke in. "Just get to work."

I lacked the will to resist them. I fell to my knees and groped in the water, studying the logs and branches on the sides of the raft until I saw one that might work to plug the opening. Taking Mayonaka in hand, I began the tedious work of cutting free a section and then shaping it. Time and again I plunged the wood into the water and felt how close a seal it made. Hours passed and the sun had already reached its summit and begun its descent before I finally fit the tapered block of wood snugly into the hole and with my failing strength pressed down and jammed it into place.

I rested back against the side of the raft. My thirst was unbearable. My tongue felt swollen. I looked at the endless waves and wondered how salt had permeated all these fathom-less depths.

"Now bail out the raft," Tex ordered.

"With what?" I protested, barely able to enunciate the words.

"You'll find something," Tex answered.

"Don't be so helpless," Tsukino-san interjected sharply.

I thought of the section of hollow trunk where I had secured Mayonaka. After freeing it from the side of the raft and removing the stopper, I began to bail. Again and again I filled this tube and tossed the water over the side. After a hundred or more times, the level in the raft looked unchanged.

"It's not working," I said.

"You're doing great," Tex opined.

"Just keep at it," commanded Tsukino-san.

I shuddered with exhaustion but obeyed. I bailed without pausing to rest or complain. At last even I could see that the water in the raft had lowered. I kept on beneath the watchful eyes of Tex and Tsukino-san. The sun had begun to set by the time I finished my work and collapsed with my head cradled on my arms.

"What are you doing?" Tsukino-san demanded.

"Resting."

"There's no time for that."

"What else can I do?"

"Prepare for rain," he answered.

"I have no containers." I could barely make my voice heard. My need to drink overwhelmed me in every way.

"You have containers," he replied calmly. "If nothing else, the raft is a container."

I saw that the raft would hold rainwater, at least until the sun evaporated what might fall on the deck. In fact, if it rained, I could spread out my cloak. By keeping the edges higher than the center, I could gather the water and funnel it into the trunk I had used to bail out the boat. I wedged the fabric into the logs, forming a corner, and drove Mayonaka into the deck to support the other side. Looking up, I saw that the moon had thickened ever so slightly and flown upward, like a silver kite, in the night sky. I lay on my back. In a few seconds the moon trembled and vanished as my eyes shut. This time I heard no protest from my friends.

Rain woke me like the touch of delicate fingers. I didn't think I could move, but at last I opened my eyes. Strange that the moon still glowed through the few rain clouds overhead. I was sure I had slept for a long while. Had twenty-four hours passed? Forty-eight? I propped myself up on my elbows. Tex and Tsukino-san were still sitting exactly where I had last seen them.

"How long has it been?" I asked.

"Drink up, partner," Tex said. "This round's on me."

Even in the moonlight, I could see the drops of water glistening on the deck. I knelt on all fours and licked the rough surfaces of the logs and occasional planks. The exquisite taste of water! I lapped in the crevices, shameless in my desire for more of the droplets. The rain lasted twenty minutes or half an hour, more a fine mist than a downpour. I freed Mayonaka and carefully scraped the liquid sheen off the fabric into small rivulets that I channeled to my tube. Having saved three or even four ounces of water, I was overcome by the irrational hope that I might live. Carefully placing the tube upright, I embedded Mayonaka in the deck to secure it in a corner.

I awoke to an inflammatory sunrise. Tex and Tsukino-san remained seated on the side of the raft.

"Are you okay?" I asked.

They didn't answer; I retreated beneath my cloak. At noon the sun made a fiery ceiling. I struggled against my thirst but finally drank the few ounces of water I had saved. Night brought relief. I begged for rain but there was none.

Another day beneath the burning sun. Now I began to see what could only be an illusion. The sun rose not once, but many times. Each sun joined the others in the sky until I no longer dared look up for fear of being blinded. More than a dozen suns had ascended in a single day. As each sun found a place above me, it burst like a nova that shone with a beautiful and destructive light. I hoped for relief if night ever came, but these shining destroyers never left the sky. I thought I could see darkness on the horizon, but I remained dwarfed beneath these brilliant lights kindled in galaxies that hurtled ablaze in the dark forever.

Still I hoped and prayed for rain. Living in this light, I had no idea how many days, how much time, might be passing. A seagull landed beside me. I wanted to dart out my hand and seize it—wring off its head and drink the blood from its neck. I ordered my arm to move, but the deserter refused to obey. I was sprawled on my back with my head propped up. The gull hopped on my stomach and swaggered to my solar plexus and then my sternum.

Looking into his dark eyes, I believed him to be a messenger. He had come from the skies. Surely he had the answers, although I had no sense of what my questions might be.

"What do you want?" I asked in a muffled, mumbling voice.

He held my eyes in a soulful gaze.

"Speak," I commanded.

With that, and without any warning or even a sign of preparation, the gull drove its beak into my cheek. Reflexively I lurched forward and the bird took flight. It didn't rush away but hovered a few feet above, where I could hardly see it because of the brightness of the sky. Tex and Tsukino-san hadn't moved, but now I saw that gulls were perched on every side of the raft. Their beaks gaped, and suddenly I could hear their frantic squawking. They waited for me, hungry and eager to strip my flesh to the bone.

At last Tsukino-san began moving his right index finger in a slicing gesture over his left wrist. I didn't understand this pantomime. I shook my head. Again he sliced the finger over his wrist, then raised the wrist to his lips.

With what felt like a superhuman effort, I crawled to Mayonaka. If I could have risen, I would have swung the blade at the gulls that watched from the perimeter of the raft like avid celebrants at a ritual. Squinting against the light, I raised my left wrist while my right hand gripped Mayonaka. I could see the blue rivers of my veins beneath the browned earth of my withered skin. My hand trembled as I brought the blade to rest against the confluence of two tributaries. Firmly I pressed until blood filled a narrow trench. Blood pooled on my wrist and glistened on Mayonaka. Careful not to spill a drop, I brought my bleeding wrist to my lips and sucked.

With my desperate thirst, this drinking of myself was infinitely delicious. My blood tasted fresh, rich, and, for want of a better word, heavy. I suckled at the gash until the blood was momentarily exhausted, then let my arm fall to replenish the supply. Again and again I did this, drinking even as I doubted that this could do more than ease my final discomfort. To the best of my knowledge, there is no such thing as a perpetual motion machine. It would violate nature's laws. If I could drink of myself and survive, gain strength, flourish, I would be as much a lawbreaker as such a machine. The wetness pleased my tongue, and I felt an energy that I suspected came as much from my excitement as from the blood trickling to my stomach.

When I could drink no more, I closed my hand around my wrist and sat propped against the side of the raft. Tsukino-san and Tex watched me without expression or movement. I kept my head bent to look away from the luminescent sky. I let my eyes close, but the crying of the gulls grew closer and more raucous. Opening my eyes, I saw them crowding toward me, dozens packed together and just out of my reach. If I stopped moving, whether to sleep or die, they would be on me in a flash.

Tex and Tsukino-san smiled at me. For whatever reason, their gentle smiles seemed to me farewells. I opened my lips to protest, feeling them my last link to human life and friendship. Tex raised his hand to stop me and pointed over my head. Then I heard bells, shifting tones of great beauty and strangeness. They played on a scale unknown to me. I turned, expecting to see the barren ocean reaching to the horizon. But there, no more than a mile away, rode the high prow of an enormous ship, its wooden hull painted gold, and the scarlet sails on its many masts puffed full by the wind and lit by the ethereal fire in the skies above. I waved Mayonaka back and forth, back and forth, with the desperation of a man who has seen his salvation and fears he may nevertheless be passed by.

Seconds became minutes. I wondered if I waved at a mirage, a phantasm that had risen from the depths. Suddenly Mayonaka slipped from my grasp. I lunged to catch it, and could only stare at the spot where the metal had pierced the soft surface of the ocean. When I raised my head, a longboat had been lowered on the swells. A scarlet banner emblazoned with a dragon fluttered above its stern. White-suited sailors dipped and pulled their oars in unison until their boat skimmed over the waves and, ever so quickly, closed the distance between us.

33

Where we found him, he could not have been. It is endless ocean. A raft might float there, but a man cannot survive. I thought him possessed because he spoke a language of the strangest sounds. But when we put water on his tongue, he drank. When we put rice to his lips, he ate. Finally I knew that this man had walked down the foaming steps to the kingdom far beneath the restless surface of the waves. There he learned a language unknown to men, a language of the secret world. Then he ascended those vast and shifting steps to return to the world above. To the rarest goods of trade, the precious gifts from mighty kings, and the celestial unicorn, I add this man, to be brought in safety to my glorious emperor Chu Ti. So will it be done.

From the log of Cheng Ho, admiral of the western seas, voyage of the fifth armada

About the Author

*T*ad Crawford's stories and articles have appeared in such venues as *Art in America, The Café Irreal, Confrontation, Communication Arts, Family Circle, Glamour, Guernica, The Nation,* and *Writer's Digest.* He is the author of *The Secret Life of Money* and a dozen other nonfiction books, chiefly on the business lives of artists and writers, and has been the recipient of a National Endowment for the Arts award. Crawford is the founder and publisher of Allworth Press. He grew up in the artists' colony of Woodstock, New York, and now lives in New York City.